CW01514047

THE SAILMAKERS

The Sailmakers

PENNY ATYEO

For my dad, Idris Jones, with love.

UPFRONT PUBLISHING
PETERBOROUGH, ENGLAND

The Sailmakers.
Copyright © Penny Atyeo 2005

ISBN 1-84426-344-4

First Published 2005 by.
UPFRONT PUBLISHING LTD
Peterborough, England.

Printed by Copytech UK Ltd.

Penny Atyeo was born in Cardiff
and grew up in Somerset.
Her parents were teachers, her father
encouraging her to write from an early age.
After bringing up a family of three
children and helping her husband with
his landscaping business she divorced.
In 1996 she went to Bath Spa University
College as a mature student, obtaining a
BA (Hons) in English and Creative Writing.
She wrote the first three chapters for her
dissertation, and her lecturer encouraged
her to continue and turn it into a novel.
She now works for a large organisation
in Somerset and has one grandchild.

I have written this novel to show how working class people from the West Country helped Britain to win the Battle of Trafalgar, one of our proudest victories. Some characters are real; others have been created by me to match the historical period, as I understand it. I am very grateful to the authors, listed at the end of the book, whose publications helped me to provide background for the period.

I am indebted to family, friends and colleagues for the help I have received whilst writing this novel.

Penny Atyeo. 2005.

Chapter 1

"Enemy fleets are out!" The weatherdeck of the Victory became thick with men staring eastwards, watching the British ships labour slowly through the waves, the prominent figureheads on their bows rearing magnificently before studding sails that were spread wide, towering over black and yellow painted high oak walls, prowling the ocean like tigers, their guns as yet unseen behind closed ports.

Fierce patriotism rose in the crewmen's chests at the awe-inspiring sight. What seaman could fail to understand the enormity of the occasion, the importance of a battle that would rid the seas forever of an overpowering foreign force? They were fighting not only for Naval supremacy but to retain their island's culture, crucial for its inhabitants' sense of belonging.

Tom Welland understood that need, along with hundreds of other volunteers; Admiral Horatio Nelson's name was being whispered reverently throughout the country, as the man whom it was hoped would lead the British fleet to victory. But he was tired; the ships' crews had endured danger and disease during months of ploughing backwards and forwards across foreign oceans, blockading ports whilst waiting for the enemy to show itself, wanting to prove that the wait had been worthwhile.

At night he prayed that he would be spared to see the family he had left behind; his son, his darling Rose, her daughter Emily and his ageing mother Mary, to whom he had entrusted the family sailmaking business in their West Country village. Coker canvas had long been recognised by the Admiralty as being of the best kind, and in great demand. Frequent storms during interminable blockading had threatened to rot the ships' sails, and as Coker cloth owed its resistance to mildew to the properties of the local water, it was ideal for the purpose. How honoured he was to be have been chosen to serve in HMS Victory, which was about to lead the British line at Trafalgar.

The sound of a drum drifted across the ocean, and in the following silence HMS Royal Sovereign fired its guns. Every man concentrated upon the distant horizon as they awaited a response from the ragged line of enemy ships, and in time they were rewarded when the Combined Fleet ran up their colours.

Would Tom see the sun set tonight, and would he live long enough to see the fleet beat the enemy and return home a hero? After all, his parish had paid a bounty to send him to sea as part of its contribution to Britain's sea force, and he couldn't bear to let them down. He had spent the previous evening at his local inn, joining brothers Seth and Alb, and Sam Fisher in a toast to the Navy, bathing in the patriotic atmosphere that had unexpectedly swept over them. And then the night before the battle the crew had lain awake in their hammocks sick with apprehension, for once the battle had started there was no way of knowing how it was going to end.

The enemy were forming themselves into the shape of a crescent, their broadsides turned towards the British, the wild but horribly bright red, black and yellow paint tantalising their opponents, their sails puffed up as they waited defiantly to come into range, firing the occasional shot which inevitably fell short.

Union Jacks and white flags had been tied to the British masts and the rigging of each ship to show their country's solidarity and determination to conquer, the massive sails arching proudly above their wooden walls. Not all Victory's crew were British; American, Swiss, Italian, German, even the French, who should have been the enemy, ranked amongst their number.

There were so many sails, it was incredible! Acres and acres of canvas, made up of long strips of cloth stitched together with twine; the thought that even a small amount of it could have been made at his ropewalk thrilled Tom, but at the same time it was terrible to know that sails made with such pride had to be used for sending men into battle.

The blue-coated, white haired figure of Nelson came into view, followed by his Captain, Thomas Hardy, and for a while he and his men appeared to be deep in conversation. Suddenly the Admiral turned and turned to speak to Pasco, the signalman, before moving out of sight.

Tom turned to the sailor standing next to him. "What d'you think he's up to?" he asked, using his hand to shield his eyes from the sun.

"I dunno," replied Richard Collins, from Philadelphia. "Fascinates me, all this strategy. We Americans think you British crazy, but so brave and loyal. Defending that little country of yours, we admire that kinda thing."

"I think the Neptune's too close," observed Tom. "Take a look behind."

The Temeraire followed HMS Victory; then came HMS Neptune, and moments later the Victory ran up Nelson's message 'Neptune, take in your studding sails and drop astern, I shall break the line myself'

All eyes were now on the leading ships, and there was a gasp as Nelson's Victory and Collingwood's Royal Sovereign swung unexpectedly off course, forming two columns and dividing the British fleet as they headed straight towards the straggling line of the enemy.

Tom stared in admiration. He had known that Nelson was intelligent, but this tactical move had been made by a man with a brilliant mind, with enough infectious self-confidence and enthusiasm to encourage his men to trust

3

him. And he trusted him completely; there was no doubt about that. This battle had been planned down to the last detail, and well in advance, of that he was certain. He guessed that Nelson had shared his plans with his officers some time before, and he was a man who had always believed that to win a battle meant taking huge risks. All the British sailors had been superbly trained; they had had more practice at sea than those of the enemy, and the Navy's gun crews were able to fire at twice their rate. The British ships would get behind the enemy and fire at point-blank range until they surrendered.

Bands were playing patriotic tunes now, and Tom's eyes began to fill with tears as he remembered his childhood, growing up in a tight-knit community, folks living in odd shaped houses in narrow, winding streets that sheltered under a hill against south western storms. In summer, threads of flax bleached in the meadows, and clumps of willows edged little wandering streams. He remembered, too, the tree in the little glade nearby that he had climbed, looking for kestrel eggs. There had been a pond where the village children fished for frogspawn and newts, its surface covered in a film of thick weed, disguising its dark and dangerous depths.

Nelson was standing on the weather deck, wearing his worn frock coat with stars of the four orders of chivalry stitched to his left breast. Clustered around him were men whom Tom recognised as frigate Captains, and after taking them on a tour of the deck he stopped to talk to the gunner.

Now the great man turned to address the six hundred men that made up the gun crews.

"My noble lads, this will be a glorious day for England, whoever lives to see it. Do not waste a single shot; I shan't be satisfied with twelve ships this day."

It seemed to Tom that the column of British ships was nearing the enemy fleet faster than Collingwood's, as if

Nelson was trying to cut the enemy off from the harbour at Cadiz. Of course! If he headed for the rear of the enemy's line he could force Villeneuve to steer away from his bolthole. The clever devil!

Now the signal 'Prepare for battle,' was raised, and within minutes the bosun and his mates were running to the hatchways shouting, 'Clear for action.'

Suddenly Tom was swept along with a tide of men hurrying to obey the bosun's shrill pipes to clear the main deck, and to take furniture and equipment down to the hold for safety. Hammocks were being taken from the nettings and lashed to the lower rigging to act as protection against musket fire; splinter nets were slung between the masts, and axes placed around the upper deck.

Tom fetched buckets of water, placing them beside each gun or near the masts, ready for drinking or fire fighting, then rolled wet canvas cloths along the orlop to the mouths of the magazines. Rope garlands were placed behind the guns, whilst men pulled down flannel screens and soaked them with water.

"Mr Willnet! Hands to Quarters. Drummer beat to Quarters!"

The drummer appeared with his heavy drum slung over his shoulders, and as the tune "Hearts of Oak" resounded across the upper deck, through the hatchways and down to the gun decks, Tom picked up extra shot and joined dozens of mates scrambling up the ladders.

Lieutenants paced the decks, keeping an eye on their men as they filled the rope garlands with shot as Willnet screeched, "All hands to Quarters, raise out there and look alive. All hands to Quarters."

Tom made for the thirty-two pounders on the lower deck, stopping at the gunner's store to collect his pistol. Hundreds of feet scurried towards the guns, and while the Captains checked their cannons, the lieutenants went to their Quarters. Once the men reached their stations the marines went to the fore and after hatches to guard them from deserters.

With a squeal the rigid port lids were raised, and Tom blinked hard, dazzled by the glare of daylight that blazed through the uncovered eyes of the ship. His gun was run forward, and he joined the rest of the team as they heaved to pull the muzzles through the ports so that their snouts poked out just above the water line.

This is more like it, Tom thought. How much better to be able to see the enemy instead of being frustrated by blindness as he worked behind the thick oak walls of the ship. Now they were ready for action.

Clouds were slowly gathering as a lieutenant made a tour of the hatchways bellowing, "Nelson has signalled 'England expects every man shall do his duty,'" through his trumpet. For a moment there was silence as the crew absorbed the information. Then cheering echoed through every deck, and within minutes the Royal Sovereign had fired the first volley. Twice more she fired, and through the thick mist of cannon fire that lay across the sea Tom watched the enemy hoist their colours

The enemies' guns flared again and again, and instinctively he ducked down behind the muzzle of his cannon as he heard the scream of shot as it pierced the foretopsail high above, for a moment losing his nerve as he considered what was to come. He was more afraid of mutilation than he was of dying, but then, ashamed of being thought a coward he rejoined the crew, working harder than he had ever worked in his life. Stripped to the waist like most of the crew, kerchief tied around his head and over his ears against the deafening pounding of the guns, Tom hurried to help load his cannon. It was hot work, and he frequently cursed the stench and wetness coming from the bilges.

At about noon, word was passed that Collingwood's column had broken through the enemy line, and forty minutes later the damaged Victory went through under the stern of the Bucentaure, firing a double-shotted broadside, as Victory 's sixty-eight pounders fired right through the enemies' stern windows.

Feverishly the crews worked the cannons, and Tom struggled to breathe as the gun deck filled with thick, choking smoke.

"Fire!"

Tom jumped back from the recoil.

The lads' bodies streamed with perspiration and dirt as again and again the guns were primed and fired as fast as they could be loaded.

As the Victory tightly engaged the enemy, Tom became mesmerised by the size of the enemy ship as it bore down upon them. Fear drove his muscles to the limit, as he helped to man the guns that showered the enemy with round and grape shot, the sailors' faces as black as the tar on their hands as they slipped and stumbled through the filth on the sodden deck.

Tom became part of the machine, leaping forward to sponge out the vast barrel of the cannon as the flannel bag of gunpowder was rammed down its muzzle into the breach, the wads and round shot being rammed in behind it. The powder monkeys came up from the magazines carrying ready filled cartridges for the thirty-two pounders, covering them with their jackets for safety, running between the cannons as the action became more aggressive.

The hammering filled Tom's head with sound, the kerchief wrapped tightly about his head and ears so ineffective that he removed it. The gun teams worked quickly, answering salvos that came rippling like thunder across the ocean, the rotten stench of powder smoke making their eyes water as it rolled heavily along the lower deck. Water oozed through the ports, and slopped about the ship as it rolled drunkenly, soaking him. His throat was parched and sore, his eyes streamed as he fumbled his way between the guns, almost rupturing his stomach as he helped to move them backwards and forwards as they were reloaded.

In his mind Tom tried to distance himself from the screams of the mutilated men dying all around him. Through the pall of smoke Tom saw the remains of bodies lying everywhere; splinters skewered men to the decks, blood soaked into the sand, and in the midst of all the horror he visualised knives and saws laid out on the sail-strewn surgeon's platform.

As he looked up, his eyes met those of the gun captain, and in the fleeting seconds that he held his gaze they shared an overwhelming feeling of utter despair.

He was brought back to the present by the clamour of the guns as they banged and flashed fire; above him carronades spewed out round shot, reminding him that he needed his kerchief; but as he was about to pull it over his head a heavy missile whipped down the length of the Neptune's lower gun deck, throwing a nearby cannon off its carriage, crushing three handlers.

A musket ball whistled past him, and instinctively his eyes followed the missile until it flicked a splinter of wood into the air, and he lost sight of it as it speared towards him, nicking his right ear. For a moment he was too numb with shock to feel the pain, but then his cheek began to throb and he screwed up his face in agony. He felt a trickle of blood against his cheek, and when he reached up to touch the wound warm blood ran freely through his fingers and onto his shirt.

The intensity of the pain enraged him.

"You bloody bastards," he screamed. "Who the hell do you think you are? You wait. We'll beat you yet, you rotten filthy foreign swine."

But he was too stunned to move. All around him frightened men were working the guns, but he was deaf to their yelling, and to the screams of the dying.

A lieutenant put a trumpet to his mouth.

"Load."

As if some mechanism in his brain had been activated, Tom leapt into action. He took a cartridge from the powder monkey, tipped it into the barrel, and the sponger rammed it home. Another wad followed and that too was rammed home.

"Run out."

The crew grabbed the gun-tackle falls and hauled until the snouts were out again.

"Prime."

Suddenly, the enemy were on both sides of them, confusing his senses. A foreign ship came alongside, and Tom looked up as a rapid broadside from the Victory's carronades ripped through its deck, emptying their squat barrels into the men ranged along the length of it, scooping them off like ninepins into the sea.

Tom could hardly see through the smoke and flames, and he was pushed aside as several of the mates flung buckets of water through the ports to put out the fires.

Faced with a solid wall of ships firing at him, Hardy pushed the Victory through between Villeneuve's Bucentaure and the Redoubtable, but as the two ships rolled in the swell of the ocean they smashed together, throwing men off their feet and guns off their mountings.

As Tom watched, the Redoubtable's rigging and sails were slashed through, planks were torn up, and now the Victory's captain seized his opportunity, ordering his gun crew to fire directly into Bucentaure's cabin windows. But now the Victory was coming into the range of the guns of the Spanish Santisima Trinidad, and a line of eight marines was mown down by a bar shot. Seconds later Victory's mizzen topmast split and fell in a tangle of sails and rigging.

Captain Harvey of the Temeraire came to Nelson's aid, opening fire upon the huge one hundred and thirty-gun ship, but a light wind caused the yardarm of the Temeraire to lock into the Redoubtable and sandwiched the French ship between the British ships. Now the French Fugue became entangled and made up the quartet of ships, all locked together.

Now Tom could see the four distinct lines of red, interspersed with ribbons of white of the Spanish ship, and as she turned, he easily picked out the ornamental group of enormous figures of the Holy Trinity at her head. As the Santisima Trinidad finally drew away, her towering sails puffed up, flaunting her state of majesty and inviting her opponents to a battle in which, despite her magnificence she was destined to become a casualty.

Time seemed to stand still as men crowding the decks of the Redoubtable queued to board the Victory, in their hands grappling hooks and grenades. Tom shuddered as a series of explosions shook the ship, and he watched in horror as his friends were picked off one by one. Wherever he looked he felt as if he were in the middle of hell's cauldron. Thundering cannons recoiled violently as the ship quivered under the onslaught as missiles flew in all directions.

Throughout it all, Tom realised, on the other side of the world life carried on normally; the sun still rose and set, at home people worked in the fields, mothers nursed their babies, and children played. How could this be real?

The Victory had suffered terrible damage; most of her masts had been shot away, sails and rigging had been cut to pieces, and her shrouds hung in confusion above her decks. The guns were run out again until they touched the sides of the Redoubtable, so close, in fact, that if any ship had fired the whole quartet of ships would have burst into flames.

As the Victory pounded the French ship, its crew trained their muskets upon Nelson's flagship from the rigging, and soon musket balls were raining down on the quarter deck as Nelson and Hardy paced leisurely across the middle of it. Nelson reached the hatchway and turned to retrace his steps, but at that moment one of the balls pierced his shoulder and penetrated his chest. He fell face down on the deck, his fate already sealed.

The smoke lay so thickly on Victory's decks that blinded men coughed and spluttered as they breathed in dust blown back through the ports. Hardy and Captain Adair came through the smoke, Hardy with a telescope under one arm, and Tom watched in horror as Adair was struck down by a musket ball slicing through the back of his neck.

The Temeraire fired a full broadside in anger, and massacred most of the crew of the enemy ship. Now Victory joined the skirmish, pointing her guns down through the enemy's hull, finishing her off. Then, as if satisfied, she disentangled herself and headed north.

As Nelson was carried down to the surgeon in the cockpit, the rest of his ships continued to battle with the Combined Fleet, their crews oblivious until the very end that their Admiral, mentor and friend, having suffered appalling injuries, was no more.

Chapter 2

The sensation was strange. Tom felt as if he were half floating, half sinking as he awoke in semi-darkness, and he shifted restlessly in his hammock. The ship lurched suddenly, reaching a new level as the currents in the ocean rose and fell beneath him; a new pinnacle was reached and for a moment it seemed as if he were poised between life and death.

He was fully awake now, holding his breath, waiting for the crash, but this time it didn't come. It had been like this for the last few weeks, as the ocean played with the towed vessel, the groaning timbers and creaking masts accentuating its hollowness. His eyes adjusted to the shadows cast by the dim lantern light, and now he was able to make out the familiar rows of hammocks suspended at either end from eyebolts in the deck head above. He wrinkled his nose; as usual the air smelt rancid, a mixture of dampness and unwashed bodies, and he recognised the familiar coppery taste that resulted from many men sleeping together in a confined space without fresh air. It would be good to see the light of day again.

Then he engaged his brain. Today they were going home. At least they'd been told it would be today, the fourth of December. Nearly Christmas too. They would be put ashore at Portsmouth soon, after several long months of patrolling the oceans, and fighting a fierce battle that had saved their country from the march of Napoleon. But the men were tired, bloody tired; they had won their battle and earned their rest, their duty done.

There was a price. There was always a price. The best Admiral lost, good seamen killed. As yet, he didn't know how many; it would be a while before they knew the total count. But one thing he knew for sure, the story of the Battle of Trafalgar would be remembered for a very long time.

"Hey, shake a leg." Harry, a man of forty, and father to the ship's boys, rolled out of his hammock, and pulled on a pair of sailcloth trousers. "Get yerselves up, no lazing around this morning. Wonder if there's time for a last swig o' rum." He grinned. "Nothing better on a cold day."

"Won't be no ale for you now, at least 'til you find the key your missus has hidden."

A gale of merry laughter floated up to the top deck, and Tom thought of the marine sentry on duty by the side of Nelson's cask, guarding his master in death as he had in life. A lonely vigil that. Perhaps he'd like some company. Anyway, he needed to take a last look at the mess of sails and masts that had suffered so much damage in the battle, and remember the friends who had died during one of the most violent confrontations at sea in naval history. He would go up later, just before they docked.

He would never forget the horrific killing and maiming and the gory remains that had littered the decks; he couldn't begin to imagine the dreadful suffering that had taken place that day. But they had beaten the Combined Fleet, and Britain had taken control of the sea. An opponent would think twice before attacking the British Navy again.

"Not much chance of any prize money," grumbled Sam Lovett, from Portsmouth, America. "Eight ships taken, and most of 'em sunk. Typical. What am I going to tell the wife?"

"That wasn't our fault!" Tom was annoyed. "The gale finished the ships off. You've come out of it well, and you'll have your pay. Money isn't everything, you know."

"Our casualties were low, considering how many thousand men the enemy lost," Jim said. "We were superb, and if it wasn't for the death of Nelson I'd say we'd done pretty well."

"Bit of a bugger, losing Nelson." A young lieutenant folded an unread letter and put it in his pocket.

"He were loyal to his crew as well as to his country," put in one of the mates, "and he were brave. I mean, who'd walk on an open deck with snipers up in the tops?"

"Without him we wouldn't be here."

Tom sat quietly, listening to all the tributes for a man he considered more than a hero. Some Admirals and captains were brutal; some sought glory, others were cold, like Collingwood. But there would never be another Nelson.

"Do you remember, after the battle," young John, another of the gunners, said thoughtfully, as he licked his fingers and snuffed out the lantern. "After Victory had been towed to that berth at Rosia Bay in Gibraltar the wounded from Trafalgar were taken to the Naval Hospital. Suddenly the Spanish were offering them their beds. What a gesture. Days before we were battering the hell out of each other. Makes you think, that. P'raps the world's not such a cruel place after all."

"Lord knows how many tears we shed that day as we carried the dead to the cemetery," Tom said quietly, stuffing his kerchief into his pocket. "And when Collingwood wanted to use the friggin' frigate Euryalus to take Nelson home we were all set to mutiny at the thought of his body falling into the enemy's hands."

"It was our job to bring him home," put in midshipman Roberts passionately, a man from Dorset, a flax weaver like himself. "We brought him out, so it was only right that we should bring him back. We would all of us have been happy to go to the bottom for him."

"Damn good job Collingwood agreed, then, weren't it lads?" Jim ran a grimy hand through the mass of curls falling over his high forehead, a glimmer of a smile showing on his well-shaped mouth. Tom pitied his wife. The man had charmed several doxies into his bed, and had never been in a hurry to throw them out again.

"I believe someone from the frigate Euryalus took the dispatches to the Admiralty," Tom said thoughtfully. "It'll take a while, I should imagine, if the carrier goes via Plymouth by post-chaise. I wouldn't be surprised if something comes out in the Gazette then and the whole country will be in mourning. Black crepe, purple drapes, ribbons, the lot."

"Surely, won't people will be thrilled by the victory? Isn't that enough?" Sam seemed surprised.

"Of course. But I think you should understand that everyone adored Nelson. He was a hero. They want to show the whole world how much they loved him. I should say he was the best Admiral of all time," Tom said quietly.

Jim changed the subject. "What plans do you have, Tom?" He ran his fingers lightly over one of the cannons, at first feeling its coldness, but under his touch it came alive again, banging and flashing fire, and suddenly he jumped away from it, as if it were real.

Tom jumped, as if he, too, felt the sensation. The memory was still too recent, the destruction too terrible to forget. It would take a while …

"To take up where I left off, I hope," he said softly. "To see my good friend Rose and my son. She will have taken great care of him, I know. And she's looking after my business," he said proudly.

Everyone turned to look at him, their voices hushed in expectation.

"I have a five year old son. Rose isn't his mother. She has a daughter of her own. Ben's mother's dead."

There were murmurs of sympathy, but Tom felt he had said too much already. His life was about to become private again. He felt an impatience for fresh air, and the need to collect his thoughts before he left.

As he poked his head through the hatch onto the upper deck, the cold wind tore through his tattered ear and he swore.

"Christ! That bloody hurts!" He whipped his kerchief from his pocket and tied it around his head for protection. Now, as he bent his head against the wind he knew he would be more comfortable below.

But it was too late; he had seen the red flash of a marine's jacket as the man left his post at the mainmast where he had been guarding Nelson's cask, and came towards him.

"Who goes there?"

"Tom Welland, volunteer, sir. Just come up for some air."

"Thought you'd be getting ready to go off."

"I wanted to take a look at the sails. See how well they've come through the journey."

Tom started to move about the deck, but the sentry moved forward with his musket.

"Don't go any further," he warned. "I know you intend no harm, but I have my orders." His voice was low and threatening.

"I could have made them sails, you know."

"Made them? I don't know about that, son. These must have been made here, or at Chatham, surely."

"I make the canvas for sails at my ropeworks at home."

"Where's home?" The sentry seemed friendlier now, his face alert with interest.

"In the West Country, sir."

"Got a family?"

Tom nodded and repeated the information he had given the seamen.

"I'm sorry."

"There's no need. It's hard for everyone. At least my son has a father."

Tom considered asking the marine about his own life, but he hesitated. There was a distance between them; a line he dare not cross.

"You must have seen us, when we were repairing the ship after the battle," he said. "Knotting and splicing, fitting runners and tackles to secure the masts. The sails and shrouds were all tangled, dirty, ripped, and shot through, little more than holes sewn together with thread. It doesn't look so bad now."

The marine shrugged and began to walk back to his post at Nelson's side, but turned suddenly as Tom spoke again.

"Did you know that these sails were sewn by hand, and sixty-four thousand yards of seaming were needed to make up one set? Not much of it left, is there?"

"That many?"

"We managed to find a spare set. The sails were old; the topsails, mizzens spritsails especially were made from double-thread canvas. Horrible journey, wasn't it, sir? Were you sick too? I've never seen a sea like it. Thought we were going to lose the masts in those heavy seas."

"I've been up here all the time, lad, watching over the Admiral. Well, off and on, anyway. I looked after him before, when he was alive."

"You see him fall?"

"No, but I was down in the cockpit, where he died."

"I heard he was brave."

"That wasn't the word for it," the marine said quietly. "I've never seen a man die with such dignity."

"Pity he didn't live to see his victory."

"I reckon he knew. Battle was over before he died."

"Nelson - he's in that cask, is he?"

"Soaked in brandy. We top it up in the aperture, and the old liquid is drawn off below."

"Strange to think of him in there, isn't it?"

For a while the two men stood in companionable silence. Above them the grey December clouds scudded by; a flurry of rain disturbed Tom's thoughts, and he shivered.

"I expect he'll have a grand funeral. None of those poor devils lying at the bottom of the sea will have a Christian ceremony with friends and family to see them off. I'll miss 'em all," Tom said gruffly.

"Me too."

"I'll stay here for a while, if you don't mind. I've got a lot to think about."

Tom sat down on the deck, his legs drawn up beneath him, his head on his knees, his eyes closed.

"Good luck with the sails."

The sentry stared intently at the young sailor, as if pondering whether to make him go back inside, but after a few moments thought, he returned to his post.

Chapter 3

Tom was standing in a field, surrounded by yards of billowing canvas, and he smiled in satisfaction. High above skylarks soared and swooped, diving low over the bright shimmering carpet of flax as it met the powder blue of the sky. The shrill screams of swifts floated in the limpid air streams, bringing the summer with them, and the first rays of the early morning sun beat down on his back, filling him with warmth and hope.

Nearby, in the long low building of the ropewalk, the spinners walked backwards for the length of it, paying out the fibre, and as the assistants turned the jack handles the hooks revolved faster and faster, and the yarn began to twist into a strand, forming the twine that would sew the sails together.

From this position Tom was able to look down on the little hamlet of West Coker. In the distance the church spire nestled between the trees, below him gangs of women lay threads of flax to bleach on the steep ridge opposite the stream. To the west, little sandy lanes wound between high hills, where coppices, fields of corn and vegetables blended into a glorious patchwork of colour.

"Ben, d'you want to see Gran?" Tom called.

His five year old son left his play and together they walked hand in hand down the track to the ramshackle shed, anxious to share their recent news with Mary, Ben's grandmother.

The door creaked as Tom pushed it open, but Mary was too engrossed in her work to notice, her head bent over her work, her fingers twisting the yarn continuously, foot tapping the treadle as she turned it into fine sailcloth. Very little light was coming from the window and she was using all her concentration for her work.

When she finally looked up Tom realised with dismay that there seemed to be a recent tiredness behind her eyes, and that the continuous lack of light had caused her skin to turn sallow Grey streaked brown hair hung lankly about her shoulders, and he knew that if he wasn't careful she would become ill from exhaustion. He felt a twinge of conscience, aware that something should have been done to help her a long time ago.

Mary's foot slowed on the treadle. "It's lovely to see you both, but I haven't got time for chattering. I've too much to do."

"You're doing too much and you need a change," Tom said firmly. "We've had an invitation from Bessie Hill. We've said you'd come. So hurry up and get yourself ready. We have to be there by three o'clock."

"Bit sudden, isn't it?"

"The Hoods have been invited."

Mary smiled. "The Captain and the Viscount? Lovely men, the pair of them. But do we have the time, Tom? Your father reckons the weather is about to change and we have a field of flax ready to be pulled. It will be a disaster if it's wet as we'll have no seed, and no fibre for spinning."

"We can't miss this opportunity, mother. Bess has a lot of influence, and these naval fellows have the right sort of contacts we need to sell our canvas."

Mary sighed and disentangled herself from the spinning wheel.

"Your father isn't too well, I'm afraid, Tom. Haven't you noticed how short of breath he's become? He's not as strong as he was and he won't be able to harvest the flax this year. With you organising the ropeworks and me the spinning, who's going to do it?"

Tom hadn't thought about that. "Maybe women in the village will be wanting work. Most of them have children old enough to help," he suggested.

"But how can we pay them? Most of our profit is being ploughed back into the business. There's nothing to spare."

"We'll have to sew one field less this year, that's all." Tom scratched his head. "It's the only thing I can think of, mother. I know it's not ideal, but we'll manage. I don't want father to worry."

"Rebecca used to help with everything," said Mary sadly. "She made such a difference."

"I miss her so much," Tom said quietly, squeezing the top of his nose between thumb and forefinger to suppress the tears that threatened to embarrass him. He considered that after five years he should have become used to her loss and learned to live with it.

Mary patted his shoulder. "I know you do, son," she said gently.

They walked in companionable silence along the little sandy lane that led to Bess's home, a farmhouse in the village of East Coker, enjoying the peace of the countryside with its familiar mixture of scents that, wherever he happened to be in the world he would remember; the strong earthy odour from the land, the sweet aroma of hazel, the reek of horse-dung, and now the pungent taste of cooking bacon that grew stronger the nearer they came to the farmhouse. And sounds like the jangling of the horse brasses as oxen ploughed the fields, the gurgling of the nearby stream as it ran behind the house, the barking of a dog, the twittering of the birds; all these things reminded him so strongly of his childhood.

"How peaceful it is," reflected Tom. "Strange to think that Napoleon's Grand Armee is encamped on the southern shore of the Channel, waiting to invade us."

"Don't think about it," Mary said quickly. "It may never happen." Her cloak caught on a sprig of hazel, and she stopped to disentangle it.

"I've heard that in some places soldiers are forming a home defence force," Tom said quietly. "They're using any old weapons they can find, drilling on their village greens, marching along country lanes. Youths are beating drums, and gathering fuel for beacons being set up around the coast. Even the old folk are busily organising everyone. The idea of an invasion is being taken seriously, mother, and I think we should listen."

"We'll see what Bess's two visitors have to say, shall we?" Mary snapped, and clamped her mouth shut, refusing to say another word on the subject.

Tom regarded her sadly. It seemed that change was harder to deal with, as one grew older.

They stopped suddenly as a family of red squirrels, noses twitching and bushy tails bobbing ran across their path, and they stayed completely still, watching them play until Ben darted forward, knees bent, hands scooped, trying to catch one of them. The squirrels scuttled into the undergrowth, reappearing a few minutes later scampering along the leafy branches of an elm sprouting in the hedgerow.

They disappeared again, and as Tom's eyes searched for them a shaft of brilliant sunlight percolated through the overhanging branches of eglantine, temporarily blinding him. He closed his eyes and let the warmth of the sun bathe his face, but then the beating of wings disturbed his thoughts, and he looked up to see rooks circling the trees in a nearby woodland before swooping down out of sight.

They continued through the lane until the hedge of hazel thinned and the track opened out into meadows; on one side of them threads of flax bleached in the sun, and on the other vegetables, flax and hemp had been sewn. Later in the season yellow cornfields would complete the colourful canvas that delightfully depicted the productivity of the West Country.

Bessie Hill, a good cook, raconteur, genial hostess, and a friend to people from all walks of life, would be waiting to welcome them, and at this time of day the kettle would be bubbling on the hook over the fire in the kitchen, her oven producing wonderful baking smells, the table set with home-made jam, cheese, bread and butter. For a while they would be able to relax and enjoy good company and perhaps make a connection or two. Later, she would fetch a bottle of wine or two from the cellar to toast her guests.

"Come along in, my dears," smiled Bess, opening her plump arms wide for Ben to leap into them. After lowering him gently to the ground, and getting her breath back, she led the way into her cosy kitchen where two men were sitting at the table, a large mug of tea in front of each of them.

Bess smiled. "I have had a little difficulty persuading Sam and Alex that my stocks of rum are depleted. Ben, my boy, you have left me a little breathless. You seem to have grown much bigger since I last saw you."

"I shall be six soon, Aunt Bess." Ben grinned, revealing the loss of two front teeth.

"What have you been doing to your father, young man?" Bess scolded, but winked at the boy to show that she was joking. "I'm sure he has more grey hairs than he did the last time I saw him."

"He wears me out," admitted Tom.

"How rude of me," said Bess. "Alex and Samuel, you haven't met Mary Welland, her son Tom and grandson Ben, have you?"

Tom shook hands with the naval gentlemen, disappointed that they were dressed casually; he had taken care to dress himself in the most acceptable manner for his ever depleting pocket; he was wearing a cut-away square-ended coat with tails, his tight fitting pantaloons strapped under his practical thick-soled leather shoes He was thrilled to be in the company of naval officers who had fought with the great Nelson, and was looking forward to an interesting afternoon.

His mother complemented him beautifully; she had wound up her hair and pushed it under a lace-trimmed bonnet; she wore a short pelisse over a sprigged muslin dress which buttoned down the front, concealing her slightly thickening figure. Tom was proud of her; clever on the spinning machine, skilful with her needle, she saved them money by making her own clothes, too. She knew how important it was to make a good impression on these two gentlemen, and that their future could depend upon it.

The younger man was tall and dignified, the Viscount shorter, his shock of white hair evident against his weather-beaten face, highlighting the lack of family resemblance; Tom was fully aware that his mother liked the way the Captain's fair hair curled softly against his cheeks, and that his eyes crinkled at the corners; he had seen her casting covert glances at him. It was obvious that, even to an older woman, a man such as the Captain would be considered most attractive.

Bess clapped her hands. "Come and sit up at the table, everyone, or else the tea will go cold. Please. Help yourselves."

As Tom had predicted, the table was groaning from homemade produce, and the conversation flowed as freely as the tea from the pot. Even little Ben behaved himself, but fell asleep half way through the meal and had to be removed to the bedroom. Tom was entranced by the tales recounted by the experienced seamen.

"Viscount Alex has just retired from the Navy, and is busy improving his home, the Cricket Lodge near Chard, together with his wife, coincidently also called Mary." Bess smiled benevolently. She was enjoying herself hugely, and in such reputable company she was certainly at her best.

"Captain Samuel has been paid off from his ship, the Venerable, so I hope this will be the first of many of their visits," she confided.

"I think I should be honest and explain that my exploits did not always turn out as I would have wished," the Captain said. "I was unlucky and lost a seventy four which ran aground. I had to strike against three French ships under Linois, but her mainmast went overboard, followed by her fore and mizzen. The enemy escaped but the crew were exhausted."

"You are too modest, cousin," smiled Viscount Alexander. "You fail to admit that as usual you led your squadron fearlessly and were thanked by both Parliament and the Admiralty. This lad will go far," he chuckled.

"Have you met Lord Nelson?" Mary enquired politely.

"I am fortunate enough to be able to call him a good friend and I am devoted to him," said Alex. "I am delighted when he can find time to visit Cricket. In the summer he and Emma adore shading themselves under my Atlas cedar tree."

"After having fought alongside Nelson I was disappointed to miss his Copenhagen battle when he beat the Danish fleet." The Captain grinned. "Would you believe, Nelson put his telescope to his blind eye, declaring he was unable to see the signal to withdraw from action. And he was well pleased when I left the Courageous, for he considered it an unlucky ship, which would doubtless have sent me to the bottom of the ocean. He is a man who really cares for his men."

"At present I believe he is fitting out Merton, in a village south-west of London, apparently an enormous task. You see," confided the Viscount, "He wants a house for Emma, a place that can be turned into a home for his retirement.

There is also the bonus of having a farm where he can indulge his passion for sheep, pigs and poultry. And of course there's always the fishing. His home is in the Palladium style, I believe."

"I have heard a little about Emma Hamilton," Mary said. "His mistress, apparently?"

"He left Fanny some time ago. Many think it an ill-considered arrangement. His little girl Horatia is looked after by her nurse in London, and of course, he misses her tremendously. Nelson considers it prudent for her to be out of the way."

Bess tactfully changed the subject. It was time for her to put into play her interest in entrepreneurial talent, which was pioneering the progress of the industrial revolution, and both Tom and his mother were aware she considered the sailmaking industry extremely important for the development of the southwest.

"Tom is a sailmaker," she said, smiling. "He and his parents own a ropewalk locally. Their Dowlas cloth is excellent. I think you will find it durable, strong and with the ability to soak up water. From what you have been telling me, gentlemen, I should think it suitable for your ships suffering from mildew, do you not?"

"Mildew has been a problem, certainly," said the Viscount. "We seem to have had more than our share of storms and gales recently. Canvas that absorbs moisture would be very useful. Why is that, Tom?"

The Viscount accepted another slice of fruitcake, but it remained untasted on his plate as he and Tom became involved in an animated discussion about the qualities of his cloth.

Bess noticed that Mary was shuffling uncomfortably in her seat, and decided to rescue her.

"Come through to the parlour, my dear," she said, slipping an arm around her guest's waist. "I want to know what you think of my new painting," Bess's eyes were alight with excitement. "I bought it in London last month. I'm told it could be a Gainsborough; it was expensive, but if it's the real thing it was worth it."

Mary tried to look as if she were impressed, going over to the painting and pretending to examine it thoroughly. It was nice, but it meant nothing to her. But then she drew back suddenly, afraid that she had damaged it accidentally, just by looking at it. Surely, grand paintings hung only in the homes of the rich, not in this one. Bess wasn't rich, and Mary wondered why she had bought it.

"Is it King George the third?" she asked uncertainly. "The brushwork has been handled delicately," she said quickly, aware that a favourable reply was expected. "And the colours have been mixed so beautifully on the palette," she added, hoping she didn't sound too ignorant.

"Stand back from it," encouraged Bess. "That's the only way a picture can be appreciated properly. That's right," she added, as Mary moved nearer to the doorway, her head tilted slightly as she reappraised the picture.

The painting in question was of a man dressed in informal coat tails with pantaloons tucked into his riding boots, holding a cocked hat in one hand, and a stick in the other. He did not look like a King at all, and as far as Mary was concerned he could have been any gentleman of the time. But Bess would not have bought a painting of any man, he had to be important, and who could be more important than their sovereign?

"It's … it's …" Mary searched for the right word, failed, took a deep breath and plunged right in. "I think this painting is majestic." She put her head on one side again, as if giving the matter some thought. "Yes," she said decisively. It's definitely majestic."

If Bess thought her opinion strange she did not show it, and flashed her most perceptive smile.

"You like it? Oh, I am pleased," she said brightly. "My father knew him, you know. He was a farmer, and the King loved sheep, so he visited our farm quite often."

Bess continued to talk animatedly, convinced that she was impressing her audience of one, but now Mary's bemused expression was changing to one of boredom.

"He comes to Weymouth too, you know. He stayed at Gloucester Lodge, and entertained two Prime Ministers, Addington and Pitt in the audience chamber of the hotel, you know. He loves bathing in the sea, and going to the theatre. But most of all he loves his family life, and is devoted to his fifteen children. He calls them his 'Cordelias,' you know. I think the royal family are wonderful, don't you?"

"Of course." Mary smiled.

Privately Mary considered Bess a little snooty, but she didn't mind. In a way she was fond of her; she had known her for many years. But she was puzzled. She was not an educated woman, but she couldn't understand why Bess had a great respect for royalty, but at the same time believed in the new industrialisation that was now spreading across the country. As she saw it, the two things would not mix, and when George the Fourth came to the throne, something was bound to change. How Tom's plans would be affected she was not sure, as he was ambitious, and already interested in one of the new machines that was coming onto the market.

With loving eyes she surveyed Tom, who was revelling in being the centre of attention. At last he was being taken seriously; someone was interested in his business, and this meeting could make all the difference between struggling and making a name for himself. But it would not happen all at once, and it would mean a lot of hard work, especially now, when he had to sell himself.

"Our canvas has an open weave with thinner threads that are more closely woven," he explained. "Double thread is our speciality, and is used mainly for the mizzen sail, topsails and spritsails. We would be delighted to show you, if you are interested."

"We may well take you up on your offer," smiled the Viscount. "And when you realise there are thirty-nine sails on each full-rigged ship, including spares, I can assure you, there's nothing better than a fleet of ships in full sail, running before the wind. Have you ever been to sea, Tom?" asked the Viscount.

Tom shook his head.

"You don't know what you're missing, my lad," he said softly. He closed his eyes, and a little smile played on his lips.

"Just imagine what it's like to go aloft, climbing through the shrouds to the topmast, trying to trap the footrope under your feet whilst holding onto the yard, then sliding down the backstay to the deck. Or furling the topgallants and double reefing the topsail and jibs, while down below the sea heaps up and breaking waves foam in a near gale. The enemy is in sight, you chase after it, the guns fire, a mast falls. Tom, you simply cannot imagine it unless you try it for yourself."

"Perhaps I shall, one day. It would be a pleasure to serve under the great Nelson, and be of assistance to my country."

The Captain chuckled. "The Hood family has the sea in its blood. My brother and I intended to destroy as many enemy ships as possible during our careers, and we haven't done too badly. Take the Glorious First of June, for instance. Two enemy ships had been disabled, and then Alex was first through the line aboard the Royal George, and disabled two more. What a blaze! I'll bet the French rued the day they met you."

"Lord Howe was knighted for that, " protested Alex.

"Do not be too modest, Alex. You won the title of Lord Bridport, and the Freedom of Liverpool. What did you do with that chain and medal you were given? I suspect it hasn't seen the light of day since."

"All that was in the past," the Viscount said, winking at Mary. "I am pleased to be retired from the madness of battle. But for your sake, Samuel, I hope we don't have to wait too long for the next one. Napoleon's army is building powerful warships, forging guns, and restocking French storehouses, although I have heard that our surplus stores have inadvertently been sold to French agents. What a shambles! The army was halved, the volunteers were demobilised, and more than sixty of our battleships were paid off."

"Everyone is emotionally aroused and waiting now that Pitt has mobilised the Government. Our Volunteer Militia are strong," Alex reminded him.

"Is it true that Napoleon can't speak a word of French?" asked Tom.

"He's actually from Corsica," replied the Viscount. "And he wants to free his countrymen from French rule. Our little Emperor intends to make Paris the centre of the world, but we're blocking his entrance to Europe, and that is why he wants us out of the way."

"Ah. Now I understand," Mary said thoughtfully. "It seems to me he thinks we are about to give in and let him take our country. If that's the case he needs to think again. We will never ever give in. I don't fancy speaking French."

"Basically we are a peaceful nation," Tom sighed. "We only fight to keep invaders out, not for the sake of battle."

"The Treaty of Amiens has given us a false sense of security for a while, and it's time we started preparing ourselves for what is to come," the Captain said softly. "France has been divided and difficult to govern since the

Revolution. Their economy has been ruined, their inflation has run out of control, its people were desperate to do away with the Aristocrats. The King was weak, so the monarchy was destroyed. People starved, lost their freedom and succumbed to terror. France became bankrupt. Napoleon came along and improved the economy and conquered much of Europe, and if we don't do something soon he will conquer us, too. That is why I am heartened to see our men arming themselves, and training so hard on their own village greens. But for quite a while now our King has been ill, some would say mad, and that son of his is so fond of gambling and women, people may think them almost an echo of King Louis and Mary Antoinette. King George is starting to age visibly and is said to be losing his sight. It seems that through illness he is becoming disinterested in politics, although he is determined to continue his country's struggle with France. If the industrial revolution produces a new entrepreneurial breed of men, powerful and aggressive, they may move away from regal control and the old feudal system. If he loses his power…"

"Are you saying that if something happens to the King we could be in trouble?" Tom asked thoughtfully.

"I don't think for a minute anything like that could happen," Alex's voice was reassuring. "We have the advantage of Horatio Nelson's expertise. So far he has won every battle he has fought. In fact, the thought of war stimulates him. He desperately wants to fight against the tyranny of a republican regime which understands only the brutality of the guillotine."

"I've heard that beacons have been set up all around the coast, and at night flames can be seen at least three miles away. Apparently the idea was taken from the Mortella Tower in Corsica which held out against the British with only three guns and a few soldiers." Tom blushed, aware that perhaps he had spoken out of turn.

Viscount Hood smiled. "Why not? If an idea works, it can be made to work again. Tom, we can learn from the experiences of others."

Bess and Mary came into the room, chattering animatedly. Bess walked up to him, took his hand and patted it affectionately.

"I was telling Mary about your home at Cricket, Alex, and the improvements you are making to the Lodge."

"Mr John Sloane, my architect, is at this very moment drawing up the plans." Alex motioned with his arm to include everyone in the room. " You must visit, all of you, when it has all been finished."

"We would be delighted, wouldn't we Tom? You would be able to bring your mother, would you not?"

"I-I'm not sure, Bess." Mary looked uncomfortable. "There is such a lot to do, what with the rain threatening to ruin the next flax crop. I don't think we shall have the time…"

"We shall find the time, I promise," said Tom. "I don't suppose the Lodge will be finished for a while, Viscount?"

"Next summer, possibly," smiled Alex. "There is so much to build; seven by six bays with a one storey Tuscan porch. Collonades will be on two of the other sides. And that is only the beginning. I doubt that I shall be spared the time to landscape it, so I can leave that to my descendants."

"Talking of descendants, dear friend, how is your nephew? I hear little Sam Hood is quite besotted with Charlotte, Nelson's niece."

"She is still at school," explained the Viscount. "It is a little too early to say, but I believe it would be an admirable match."

"They'd love Cricket," enthused Bess. "It's so peaceful there. Away from London, and all that dirt and smoke. Servants to pamper you, time to relax, and the Viscount knows so many people. It's only about twelve miles from here, and in good weather it's possible to see Beer and the bay of Seaton, which opens into the English Channel."

"Ah, I can see why Nelson is attracted to it," Tom commented. "He would feel quite at home there, sitting amidst acres of land, overlooking the Channel, keeping an eye out for the enemy."

"Not so long ago highwaymen patrolled the long open Turnpike Road between Crewkerne and Chard," Bess said.

"But Cricket is in a valley," protested the Viscount. "And that was a long time ago. The little church and its tiny graveyard is well worth a visit." He covered his mouth with his hand to stifle a yawn. "Please excuse me. I do not mean to be rude, but I'm afraid old age is taking its toll, and I shall soon be thinking about leaving."

"It has a little wooden font, you know," interrupted Bess, once again anxious to impress. "And outside there is a turret with three bells. Very pretty. Just the setting for a wedding. You're walking out at the moment, aren't you, Captain? I'm sure…"

Samuel Hood stood up, and replaced his chair under the table, and kissed Bess on the cheek.

"Regretfully we have to take our leave, Miss Hill. Thank you for a wonderful spread. Alex and I are due at the Admiralty shortly, and we have to travel to London." He held out his hand. "It was good to meet you, Tom and Mary. And good luck with your twine works. I have a mind to speak to our Naval Inspector. That Dowlas cloth you mentioned sounds as if it might be just the thing to combat our mildew problem."

Chapter 4

Tom glanced out of the kitchen window when he heard tuneful whistling coming from the lane behind his cottage, and he hurried to collect his coat to join the flax pullers as they came through the early morning mist.

The men carried pitchforks, followed by their families; the older children running in front, mothers with their babies lagging behind, older folk anxious to earn a few pennies for the winter. Tom had promised them extra pay if they worked quickly, and without grumbling. He looked up at the sky, and was relieved to see that, for the moment, the skies above them were perfect for harvesting the flax, but they would have to hurry, for the gathering winds were blowing through the tall stalks shaking out valuable seed, and in the distance dark thunderclouds were creeping over the horizon.

His father, James, had taken to his bed with a harsh cough, and Mary had given him strict instructions not to rise from it until he felt well again. He had known better than to disobey and anyway, she had ignored his weak protests, kissed his pale cheek, drawn the sheets up to his chin, closed the curtains and left him to sleep.

She ran downstairs to help Tom load baskets of food for the villagers' mid-day break onto the wagon. Then she passed little Ben to his father and jumped up beside them both as Tom took the reins, clicked his tongue to the mare and swung the wagon out into the lane. Soon they were overtaking gangs of labourers as they hurried to avoid a heavy downpour.

The flax had grown straight and tall, and now that the pretty blue flowers had fallen, and the seed capsules had turned from green to brown, it was ready to pull. The men had stripped off their shirts and started work, the muscles in their arms rippling as they pulled the plants up from the roots, taking care to keep the stalks parallel. Each handful was laid on the canvas, each one being set parallel to the other about a foot or so apart. The next handfuls were laid across these until they formed a small pile about three feet high.

Usually it took several days to harvest the whole field, but now the future of the business depended upon the labourers' hard work to bring in as much of the flax crop as possible before the first drops of rain began to fall.

"Come on, help me," panted Tom as he ran around the canvas, folding in each corner around the precious crop until the plants were covered. "We have to get this inside."

The men came to help, sharing the weight between them as they loaded the sailcloth onto the cart.

Then the storm started, slowly at first, and the rain was falling in sheets as Tom drove the cart into the barn. He peeled back the canvas and inspected the plants, and to his surprise he realised that the rain had done very little damage at all.

"It doesn't look too bad," he said. "Let's get this canvas onto the floor, and the women can take over."

The men gathered around the canvas, grabbed the edges and heaved.

"Try to hold it steady," Tom said. "Now lower it gently. That's right." And under his guidance the load settled comfortably onto the barn floor.

"Thank you everyone," Tom said "Very well done. There you are, Bess. Would you like to take over now?"

Bess had offered to organise the rippling. Not yet forty, she was nimble on her feet, and competent, as she had been helping with the harvest since childhood. The rippler, a comb set in a wooden frame with round iron teeth eighteen inches long, had been set in the centre of the sheet, and now the women stood either side of it, pulling the stalks through the teeth, separating the seed heads from each stalk.

A large bird suddenly swooped low from the rafters and flew like a whisper around the roof of the old barn, startling the women working below, and disappeared into the loft above, only to dislodge a colony of sparrows that flitted in and out of the eaves.

Outside the air was filled with women's voices singing in harmony as they worked, the sound rising through the oaks and elms above scrubland where children made their dens. Brown chafers swarmed about the poplars, the quivering of their silver backed leaves impressive against the overcast sky, finally floating down over the fertile, well-watered meadows where flax seed had first been sown in the spring.

The retting pond had now been dug, and Tom had employed several men from the village to dig the trench.

"It must be deep enough now," Harry said, as he walked up and down the trench, measuring the distance with his feet.

"It should be fifty by nine, and ten feet deep," he murmured. "We're nearly there. Another couple of feet should do it."

The pond had been filled with water, and now that the weather was warm enough it was time to start the process of soaking the stalks until they rotted. The labourers began the laborious task of tying them into sheaves and packing them into the pond, roots downwards, weighing them down with planks and stones to start the fermentation process.

Out in the field, the women were laying out a picnic, but several of the older children had slipped away unnoticed, and were now clustered excitedly around the pond, waiting for the bubbles to appear.

"Come away from there, it's dangerous." Tom shouted, and chased them away, but the children kept returning, finding the whole event fascinating.

"For God's sake." Mary pulled one of the boys away and clipped him around the ear. "Do you want to drown in there, you stupid boy?" she snapped. "And you others. Get back home this instant, or I won't be answerable for you."

"This is ridiculous," shouted Bess, as she handed a little girl back to her mother for the fifth time.

"Haven't you warned her to keep away from water?" she asked the woman crossly. "You should know better."

"I can't watch her all the time," the woman mumbled.

"I'm afraid you have to, that's what mothers do."

Bess walked away, shaking her head in bewilderment.

"Why is it that some mothers can't seem to look after their children properly?" Tom sighed. He was sitting on the old settle by the fire, with his feet on a low table, a pint of cider in his hand. Mary looked up occasionally from her sewing to answer him.

"There are retting ponds and streams for miles around. Hundreds of them. And none of them have been fenced off. Retting is a very necessary part of the process of sail making, and if neither you nor Bess had been there I dread to think what could have happened. We should have moved that pond away from the field a long time ago."

"Do you know," Tom said thoughtfully. "Here we are, considering the fact that the majority of our village children can't swim, when one day soon I may be joining the Navy as a volunteer. I can't swim either."

"I shouldn't think it'll matter whether you can swim or not," Mary said logically.

"I haven't wanted to think about it," Tom replied, staring out of the window into the garden. "Look at those birds fighting over a worm. Everything seems so normal. Bad things happen, but life goes on."

Mary surveyed her son, lines of worry etched deeply on her forehead, and her voice trembled when she spoke. "You will take care, won't you, son?"

Tom turned to face her.

"I'm so lonely," he murmured. "Would if matter if I was killed fighting for my King and country?"

"I can't bear it when you speak like that," Mary said softly. "You need company, son. Do you ever think you might meet someone else?"

"I shouldn't think so," Tom said gloomily. "I don't think I'll ever get over losing my wife."

For a while Mary said nothing, for there was nothing left to say. Suddenly she stood up and started clearing away the supper.

Tom went to bed, and dreamed about retting ponds, drowned children, and Rebecca.

Two weeks later, Tom visited the pond for the last time to test the condition of the stalks, and found that at last the fibre had separated from the bark, although the gum surrounding them needed to be washed out in the stream.

Again the labourers were called upon, and Harry and George organised labourers, wagons, and carts to spread the bundles around the field to dry. Tom looked up at the clear blue sky, noting with relief that no rain clouds were in sight, and prayed that it would remain that way for the next two weeks.

Tom watched the women laying the threads of flax to dry, turning his head so that he could look down over the little hamlet of West Coker. He picked out the church spire of St Martin's nestling between the trees, and the enormous yew growing by the church porch.

His eyes misted over at the memory of Rebecca walking down the aisle of St Martin's, especially the piece of pink lace that had been pinned onto the scooped neckline of her white muslin dress. He reached into his pocket and drew out the fragile snippet of lace, pressing it against his face, trembling as her fragrance surrounded him, bringing back all the joyous memories of that day. Golden curls had been swept up on top of her head, braided with pink ribbon, accentuating that wonderful, kissable slender neck Where was that ribbon now? He should have it with him. Desperately he searched his pockets, but it was not there.

Suddenly the sun faded, and he sweated and then shivered in panic as he looked about him in despair. How could he have lost it? That ribbon had been with him for the past six years. Oh God, where was it? He looked down. Suddenly, there it was, floating down the hillside towards the women laying out those threads of flax.

So he ran, tripping over his feet as he almost fell down the hillside towards that little piece of pink ribbon that fluttered enticingly before him in the wind. Then it was in his hand, and he was crying, with all those women watching him, but he had found it, and that was all that mattered. As he made his way home, he couldn't resist one more glimpse back at the church, but it was long enough for him to hold onto his dream. His emotions were raw as he saw her again, this time with her bouquet of snowdrops; it was early spring, and he had picked them for her the day before. She had emerged from St Martins looking radiant; the sun had appeared through the clouds at just the right moment to cast a glow over the wedding party. The fiddler had struck up a lively tune, and they had danced down the path, crunching freshly strewn berries and rushes underfoot as they made their way towards the old yew tree at the gate.

He should have known then that the shadow that had partially covered the horned window in the tower would be a bad omen; shortening the time he would have with his new wife.

Why had he remembered all this today? Was it Rebecca's way of telling him to move on, to let her go, to be happy with someone else? His mother thought he should. She had mentioned it to him several times; no doubt when she thought he would be receptive to the idea. She was keen for him to have someone in his life again, especially for Ben, for should anything happen to him the boy would not be alone. She had not intended to hurt him, but he was not ready for that.

With such thoughts on his mind, Tom made his way back to the Ropewalk, and, slipping in through the side door, silently watched the rope maker and his assistant prepare to make the twine. The spinner checked the condition of the yarn, then, the fibre around his waist, he raised his hand to tell the assistant he was ready. He began to move backwards slowly along the walk, and the assistant started turning the crank handle to twist the yarn into twine. The strands were contracting when the door opened and Mary came in. She walked towards her son and whispered something in his ear.

Abruptly Tom followed her outside, and together they ran down the lane towards the flax field.

"I thought they'd emptied the pond," he panted, as he ran through the gate, leaving it swinging behind him. "Who's child is it?"

"Rose Howard's little Emily." Mud clung to their boots as they made their way slowly towards the corner of the field, where several labourers had gathered around the pond.

"How old is she?" Tom was busily cutting a branch of hazel sprouting from the hedge.

"About six, I should think. She lost her little sister through measles last year."

He nodded. He remembered the measles epidemic. Ten children had died, and the village had been in mourning for months. For this to happen to the same family…

"We should have drained that damn retting pond," he said, voicing his mother's thoughts.

"Be fair, Tom. We haven't had a chance. We've been busy lately."

"That's no excuse," Tom growled. "We knew the risks." He assessed the length of the branch, and then whittled away loose twigs from the base.

"At least we should have given our workers the time to do something about it."

"But would they have?"

"We're not going to lose this child," Tom said grimly. "Let's hope this will be strong enough."

"Let's hope she hasn't gone under the water," Mary said quietly. "I don't think I could live with myself if she died."

"She's not going to die," he snapped "There's no need for you to get involved, mother. I don't want you getting hurt. I'll deal with this."

"I am involved, whether you like it or not."

As they drew nearer, Rose ran towards them, and Tom could see that she was shaking uncontrollably, her arms a mass of scratches and bruises where she had tried to rescue her daughter. He looked down into her tearful face and felt a sudden surge of emotion, and it took him by surprise.

Desperately the woman clung to his sleeve. "Get her out, please, Mr Welland, she pleaded. "She's been under once already. She can't swim. I intended to teach her, but she's the only one I've got now. Please. Don't let her drown."

"Try not to worry, she'll be fine," he said gently.

Swiftly he assessed the situation, then removed his coat and strode purposefully to the edge of the water. As he reached into the murky depths several feet below, the labourers gathered around the pond, watching his attempts to grab the child, who seemed to be trapped between two wooden planks, her nose only an inch or so above the water. Her arms were thrashing wildly, and Tom guessed that she was trying to release her feet from the stones that were trapping her, and he could see she was tiring.

"Make room," Tom said, as he got down on his knees by the edge of the pond. "Pass me that branch, please mother."

"Don't be frightened Emily," he said calmly. "All you have to do is to hold tight and I'll try to pull you out."

Emily grabbed the branch, and Tom pulled, but nothing happened. Others watched helplessly, and it soon became obvious that if her legs were not freed, she would drown, and in desperation Tom threw the branch aside and jumped into the pond.

Tom disappeared from view, and the labourers gasped. He was finding it difficult to gain a foothold, his feet slipping and sliding over the slimy wood, and for Mary and Rose the waiting was terrible. But then two heads bobbed up, and Tom reached out for the branch that would take them to safety.

Emily lay on the ground, her face covered with mud and grass, seemingly lifeless. Everyone leaned over her anxiously, watching for a sign that she was alive.

"Emily, are you all right?" screamed Rose, pushing the labourers away as she knelt by her child's side, frantically tearing the muck away from her face, then cradling her head in her arms, her face white with fear. Emily had stopped breathing, and instinctively she rolled her daughter onto her side so that the water could run out of her mouth.

"Come on, breathe, sweetheart," she pleaded. "I need you to live. You're so young, and you have so much to look forward to."

Tom, dripping with water, clambered out of the pond. A single glance was enough to make him aware of Emily's plight; he gritted his teeth with grim determination and staggered towards her. This accident had been his fault, his alone, and if he had caused her death he would never have forgiven himself.

Rose saw him coming, and her relief was tangible as he dropped down by her side and started to work on Emily, breathing life into her. Suddenly the little girl spluttered, and her eyes flickered open.

"Sweetheart. You're all right!" she gasped, holding her close.

"Let me take her inside into the warm," offered Sam Parsons.

Gratefully Rose allowed him to take her child from her, but her eyes followed their progress until she was safely back at the door of the cottage.

Ecstatically, Rose stood up and kissed Tom on the lips, and now he could see that her eyes were brimming with tears. "I don't know how to thank you," she cried. "I really thought I'd lost her." Then, as a new thought occurred to her, she said, " I hope she hasn't spoiled all your work, sir. I don't know how she got in there."

"Bother the flax," Tom said slowly. His lips were tingling from the touch of her lips, which, although brief, had sent shock waves through his body, and from her expression, he could see that the brief kiss had affected her, too. It was now that he knew he might have to reconsider a promise he had made to himself the moment his darling Rebecca died.

Chapter 5

Tom's father James recovered enough to work at his loom again, and despite pleas from his wife not to over exert himself, the old man was determined to help, and wouldn't listen.

Tom determined to keep an eye on him, visiting his workshop frequently, taking him soup or broth to sustain his strength, and chatting to him to keep up his spirits. The previous evening a cough had accompanied the clicking of his handloom, and aware that his father did not take easily to his bed, Tom decided to drop in to see him the following morning after breakfast.

Now, as he walked down the path a short way from the cottage and heard the reassuring click of his father's loom coming from the shed, he reckoned that either his father had decided on an early start and an early finish, or was obstinately driving himself on without a thought for his health.

Tom worked his way around the tangle of brambles until he found the door and let himself in.

James was sitting on a low stool weaving sailcloth from a bundle of yarn, pedalling his legs furiously as he worked his loom.

For a while Tom observed him without speaking, noting with guilt the furrowed lines that had recently appeared between the strands of lank grey hair on his forehead, the hands that shook as they worked the yarn, the sweat that occasionally dripped from his brow onto the cloth, and it was now that he realised how much he loved him. This was a man who had never had much, had worked all his life for all he owned, and, like most of the labourers in his village, his face was heavily lined, giving him an appearance of an exhausted old man. It was time to make life easier for both his parents.

James Welland glanced up briefly when his son entered, and his eyes lit up when he saw that Tom had brought more yarn.

"Lay it down by the side of that lot," he said, indicating a pile of cloth on a chair in the corner. Your arrival is very timely," he said gruffly. "As you can see, I've finished the last bundle." James put his board under his workbench and tidied away a knot of loose yarn before standing up stiffly and stretching.

"I reckon there should be enough for Russell's Carriers to take to London," he said proudly. "I've been told it's every bit as good as Haywards.' In fact, it may be better. I don't hold with competing with any other of them West Country sailmakers."

"We have to," Tom said gently. "When we have regular customers, possibly from further afield, we'll need enough to go around. That will be the future, father. We are entering an era of industrialisation, when machines will take the place of man. All the young people are talking about it. There is a gentleman near Bridport who owns a swingling mill and his flax comes by sea to the harbour. He had the foresight to harness water to drive the wheel at his mill, and he's doing very well, I believe. He buys in the raw material, which goes to the mill and warehouse where it is made ready for spinning on his premises, or returned to other manufacturers. You probably remember that not so long ago people from our local villages spun hemp into yarn and sent it to Bridport for them to manufacture cordage. As you know, yarn comes from all over; East Coker, Yeovil, Viney

Bridge at Crewkerne, West Chinnock - there are many more - and with canvas used for so many things now it's always going to be in demand, so you needn't worry."

James turned to his son with tears in his eyes. "But I do worry, son. Us old 'uns don't like change. It scares us. We don't understand it. Our Dowlas cloth has always been the best, and the reason is due to the Cokers' spring water, everyone knows that. We should be holding our heads up high and striding ahead of the field.

"But it doesn't matter," Tom said quietly. "There is enough room for us all. I believe that competition is good. It makes businesses try harder, and although profits may be shared it ensures the best products will be made, and Britain will benefit. Isn't that what it is all about?"

James frowned. "We may find that none of us are needed any more, as bigger mills and industries take away our living."

"I have to disagree with you there, father, as I believe in progress," Tom said firmly. "And without it we cannot move on."

"Naturally. But until village labourers can afford to pay for this new machinery, they may find they lose their jobs."

"I hate to disagree with you again," said Tom, "but I think you'll find that the mills in the north are already becoming industrialised, and the coming war with the French will make a difference. There are new economic opportunities coming, and I believe that we can combine local businesses. If we don't make a place for ourselves in the world we shall be left behind. One day you will realise it, father."

James sighed, and dropped down into his tattered wicker chair. "Oh, I will be dead and gone by then, long gone," he said, staring into space. When he spoke again his voice was strained, as if he were finding it hard to control his feelings.

"I dare say I won't have to worry about it. I've had my battles with the enclosures, and they were bad enough."

"Come on father, it's not as bad as that! Every generation has its problems, you know. But the future looks bright, and I for one am very excited by it."

His father looked up at him and now Tom thought he detected a hint of a smile on his lips. Perhaps his old man was playing a game with him to see whether he could trust him with his business when he was gone.

Now the old man leaned back in his chair, raised his arms, interlocked his fingers and tucked his hands behind his head. "My father once told me that hemp and flax were grown locally as early as thirteen hundred and nine, and fifty years later it was sent to Bridport. From then on it was cultivated all over the South West. So I suppose," James paused for a moment as his wife entered with two mugs of soup, "if the industry has been going for all those years there's no reason to suppose that it should stop now."

"It hasn't been easy dear." Mary cleared a place for the steaming mugs on the workbench. "Remember that year of the drought when nothing grew, or the bread riots when we were close to starving? Those were hard times. Mind you, I wouldn't like to have been living in France over the past few years."

"Bess reckons that Madame la Guillotine has been very busy lately. I'm glad our country isn't so barbaric. It must have been terrible living under such a regime," Tom said thoughtfully.

The men sipped their soup in silence, their heads bowed in thought, while Mary swept the floor and piled the cloth into a box and closed the lid, ready for the carrier when he called the following Tuesday.

"Why don't you two men take yourselves out into the garden for some fresh air while the weather's nice," suggested Mary. "Then I can have a good tidy up."

"What is it you want to do here, Tom?" asked his father, as they walked up the path towards the cottage.

"Go mechanised."

"How would you do that?"

If Tom was encouraged by the note of curiosity in his father's voice he tried not to show it He looked up into his face, his eyes alight with enthusiasm.

"If we could afford Cartright's new power loom our yarn would be finer and because it's faster we could turn out twice as much as we do now."

"Any drawbacks?"

"Not really. What I do like is that the flax has to be drawn out into slivers and twisted, ready for the machine, rather than combing out the fibre to draw out the longest pieces, as we do now."

"Any other ideas?"

"A new workroom. With high, wide windows along each side so that the workers will be able to seam the sails until the sun goes down. That's what's happening in all the larger mills; labourers with permanent wages, more land to grow the flax, and…"

James held up his hand. "Stop. Don't get carried away, son. These ideas are all very well, but where's the money coming from to carry them out?"

"I don't know, yet," Tom admitted. "But I do have the determination to make it happen."

James shook his head. "That may not be enough."

Tom looked down at his shoes, noting that, like the rest of him, they had become shabby. He had always tried to stand apart from the labourers, but now he realised that with his rough shirt, fustian jacket and plain sailcloth trousers he had now become one of them. If he were to gain respect he would have to take responsibility for not only himself but for the rest of his family, and if he was to impress Rose he needed to buy some new clothes and get a shave and a decent haircut. The moustache he had started to cultivate would have to go. Then, he thought boldly, he would set about asking her out, and trust that she would be pleased to accept his invitation.

Perhaps she would help to smooth out his rough edges to make him into the caring man he had been when Rebecca was alive, but she could only do it if he allowed her to. He barely knew the woman he had met only a few days before, so how could it be that whenever he thought of her his heart pounded and he felt breathless as if he had been running up a hill? And would he ever be able to ignore pangs of guilt every time he thought of her?

"Do you know a lady called Rose Howard?" Tom asked, as they stopped by the gate so that he could slip the piece of twine over the post.

"The young woman who nearly lost her child in the pond?"

Tom nodded. "That's the one. What d'you know about her?"

"Lives somewhere up by the church in East Coker, I think. Near the Almshouses. Lost her remaining daughter and her husband the same year."

"Lost her husband too?" Tom's mouth went dry. The poor woman! He'd presumed…what had he presumed? He should have realised there would be a husband. What was the matter with him? He should never have been thinking of befriending a woman who had been through all that.

"Why do you want to know?"

"Do you know all the labourers who work for you?" Tom snapped.

James raised his eyebrows. "What's the matter, Tom?" he asked bluntly. "Fancy her, do you?"

Tom said nothing.

"You do, don't you? Come on, Tom. You like Rose Howard. There's nothing wrong with that."

"She's only lost half her family," Tom said miserably. "And I've lost Rebecca."

"So what."

"So what?" Tom turned on his heel and started to walk away, but James caught his arm and brought him back.

"Maybe two lonely people ought to get together and keep each other company, that's so what."

"I can't do that to her." Tom's voice sank to a whisper.

"Maybe she wants company. You won't know unless you ask her."

"I don't think…"

"All I know is that I am an old man with not very long left, and I would like to see my son settled before I die. I'm sure that goes for your mother as well. I think you should go and see her. How else can you find out?"

The air was fresh, and only a few light clouds puffed their way across the sky as Tom stood by the place that had once been the retting pond. Although it had been filled in the sight of it still sickened him. But it had been the catalyst that had led him to Rose, and for that he had to be grateful.

Swiftly he moved on down the hill, and upon reaching the crossroads in the centre of the village he took the turning to the right, which led to Yew Hill Rocks at the bottom of Primrose Hill. Thick mud from the drying ruts of Halves Lane clung to his boots, making it hard to walk, and he was relieved when he turned off the track into East Coker.

Ahead of him the light streamed through branches heavy with hazel nuts, and his ears were filled with the noisy chiff chaffs as they chattered to each other through the undergrowth. He paused for a while, watching thrushes beating snails against sharp pieces of stone, leaving a sea of shells littering the ground. The grass covered banks were full of holes where house martins had taken advantage of the soft earth, and he looked up from this familiar country scene to where a stream flowed into the valley of East Coker along Slaford Bottom, where in summer as a child he had often swum naked. From there it flowed eastwards past East Coker Mill, through Pavyott's retting ponds, then away towards Barwick and to the River Yeo.

Tom closed his eyes and sighed with pleasure, absorbing this glorious part of the West Country he called his own; in every direction a scene evoked colourful memories that he would cherish until his dying day. If only he could stay here forever, cocooned in the tranquillity of the little copse.

Surely, he thought, that tree he climbed looking for kestrel eggs would be around here somewhere. There had been a pond too, he remembered, where the children of the village had come to fish for frogspawn and newts, its surface covered in a film of thick weed, disguising its dark and dangerous depths. In winter they had skated on its icy surface, but in those days danger had been the attraction. He shuddered. He wouldn't go looking for trouble.

In spring sunshine yellow daffodils and crocuses clustered around the foot of an old oak trunk, the more delicate celandines and primroses growing in drifts throughout the wood. This was the perfect place to bring Rose. He smiled. Emily and Ben would love it too. They could bring food, and lay it out on the sparse grass, but they would not be allowed to roam too far. That terrible pond would never claim their children.

Back Lane was as steep as he remembered, and by the time he reached the top he had to stop to catch his breath. He was not far from the Almshouses, so Rose wouldn't be far away. He acknowledged a couple of old men, their chins propped up by the handles of their brooms as they rested under the beeches from their daily round of sweeping the road.

In the valley below gentle rays of sun slanted through the windows of the yellow ham stone cottages, stone that had been quarried locally from Ham Hill. Thatched roofs had been finished neatly with the thatcher's emblem where Bess's house nestled comfortably amongst clustered canopies.

He could see the road that ran past the forge, rising again to where the horizon met the sky, the tiny wandering clouds making a scenic backdrop for the great oaks and chestnuts. In the foreground the pasture was set out like a colourful chessboard. To his right lay the marshland with its elder and willow thickets, where in autumn the river flooded the road; beyond, Pincushion Corner led to Closworth, Halstock and Sutton Bingham.

Behind him was Coker Wood, full of oak and ash and sweet chestnuts, where clumps of primroses and bluebells emerged in spring under the hazel hedges and in the ditches, and in the summer roe deer roamed freely, their mottled backs blending into the leafy shadows of the wood.

He came to a little cottage set well back from the road, and there was something familiar about its appearance, as if he was well acquainted with the person who lived there, perhaps in the way the ivy covered the door, or the honeysuckle that rambled in the hedge, even the net curtains at the windows that gave it a homely appearance.

A child opened the door, and immediately it was evident that she did not recognise him. Tom didn't recognise her either. The half drowned waif that he had rescued that day was indeed a beautiful little girl; long lashes framed her deep blue eyes, and her thick blond hair was tied in a loose knot and hung down her back. Even her mouth, trembling with uncertainty, was well-shaped. She walked barefoot, her voluminous smock concealing her thinness.

Rose came to the door with a spindle in her hand, and upon seeing Tom she looked down at her dress in dismay, quickly slipping a wayward button back into its hole at her breast. She blushed in embarrassment, but then stood back, allowing Tom to enter the small living room. Emily went to sit on a low wooden bench, next to the inglenook, where logs burned in the large open fireplace.

"I didn't hear you. I'm sorry. I was out the back." She held out her hand for his coat. "Come and make yourself comfortable please, Mr Welland," she said, indicating the settle drawn up in front of the fire.

"I hope you don't mind the intrusion," Tom said, as he removed his coat and handed it to her.

"It's good to see you." Rose hung the coat on a peg in a corner of the living room. "I must apologise that I haven't been to thank you before now. It's very rude of me."

"I'm pleased to see how well she looks."

Tom addressed the child. "I hope you feel better now, Emily."

The child's lip quivered, and she looked to her mother for guidance. Rose smiled and nodded encouragingly, then after a few moments thought Emily smiled warily, but remained sitting, finally turning her attention to untangling a knot of yarn, her long nimble fingers carefully teasing each strand apart.

"She has a bad dream occasionally," Rose said softly. "Apart from that, as you can see, she's fine. I really am most grateful to you."

Rose smiled shyly, and Tom's heart contracted painfully. Her lips were tantalisingly close, and he desperately wanted to kiss her again. He was aware of the tantalising smell of her skin, the softness of her hair, the sound of her voice, and he was finding it hard to keep his distance. He wanted to show her how he felt, and to ask her if she felt the same. But then, as if reading his mind, she turned away from him, took two mugs down from the shelf and put them on the table. She opened a little box, measured out the tea and spooned it into the pot. She took the kettle from the trivet.

"Would you like some tea? I'm afraid it'll be weak, but at least it's hot. I'm afraid I have nothing else to offer you."

He nodded and she raised the kettle to pour the water onto the tea, but as she did so she glanced up at him, and the expression in his eyes seemed to unsettle her. For a few moments the kettle remained poised above the pot.

"I'm sorry." Tom realised he had been staring at her, and turned away in embarrassment." I didn't mean to…"

The tea splashed into the cups.

Rose spoke quickly. "I wish I had some cake to give you, but I haven't had a chance…"

Tom doubted that she had eaten cake for a long time. "I don't want cake," he said softly. "I'm grateful for the tea, especially after the long walk up Back Lane. You're very kind."

A swift look around the room had already confirmed his suspicion that Rose was struggling to make a living for the two of them. The only other pieces of furniture were a table and a three legged stool; three shelves holding some of her household bits and pieces, and possibly a few possessions were kept in the cupboard under the stairs. He presumed there was a back kitchen, as there were no cooking utensils on show. Flagstones covered the floor. There were no rugs.

There must be a solution, surely, he thought. Women like Rose, and children like Emily worked long hours in their own homes making cloth, sewing gloves, taking in work whenever it was available. It was plain that she was poor, and he wondered whether she had been a poor wife or had become a poor widow upon her husband's death. She needed help, but was he the one to give it?

The table was full of clutter; pieces of canvas, twine in various shades, a spindle whorl, loose yarn; the hand loom in the corner, told him that he was encroaching upon this woman's valuable time. The longer he stayed the more money she would lose, and he started to feel guilty. He was aware, too, of the presence of the child in the room, but he could hardly ask Emily to leave so that he could be alone with her mother.

Tom was in a dilemma. The only thing he could offer and hope Rose would accept was his friendship.

"Would you mind if I came again?"

"No!" Emily ran to her mother and hid in the folds of her skirt.

"She doesn't like sharing me," Rose explained. "She's had a hard time, losing first her sister, her father, and then the trouble at the pond. I think she's afraid she'll lose me, too."

"I'm sorry, Emily," Tom said gently. "I didn't mean to upset you. It's just that I have a little boy called Ben. He's about your age, and I know he'd love to play with you. Would you like to meet him?"

Emily smiled nervously, and whispered to her mother.

"She's not sure. She needs time to think about it."

Tom nodded and smiled at her. "That's fine, Emily. I understand."

"I have to make some rushlights, or we'll have no light for tonight." Rose indicated a pile of clothes stacked in a corner. "And I need to see to do the mending as I have to keep us looking decent. Emily. There's a pile of rushes in the yard. Perhaps you'd fetch them for me."

Her daughter put down the knot of yarn and went out into the back yard. Seconds later she came in carrying a bundle of rushes and put them on the table.

"Can I watch?"

"Course you can watch, Mister. You can help if you like."

Rose fetched a knife from a pot on the shelf, picked up one of the rushes and snipped off both the ends, leaving only the pith. She handed him the knife.

"The green skin has to come off, except for this little strip of skin." She eyed him critically as he obeyed her instructions.

"Now it's my turn." Emily fetched a tin, dropped in a lump of fat, and set it by the fire to melt.

"What happens now?"

"She puts the rushes into the grease to soak, then they're taken out and put into a small piece of bark. Then I fasten them together and strap them up against the wall until I need them. Surely, you must have made rush lights before, Tom." Rose's voice held a note of incredulity.

"'Fraid not. We use candles. They don't smell, and they last longer."

"D'you make candles, Mr Welland?" Emily was looking at him with renewed interest.

"I do," Tom said, looking down at the child that only a few moments ago was eyeing him with mistrust. "They're easy to make, Emily. All you do is to pour the grease around a wick in a candle mould. I you like, next time I go into town I'll get you one."

The garden gate clanged, and someone ran up to the front door and banged on it loudly. Rose was about to answer it, but Tom was there before her. He had recognised Johnny, his spinner, as he passed by the hedge, and guessed that something was wrong.

"Your father's very ill," Johnny gasped, and then collapsed against the door, his face ashen, his breathing rapid.

"Bring him inside." Rose cleared a space on the settle and Tom lowered the old man onto it, his head resting uncomfortably on one ledge, his feet on the other. Johnny closed his eyes and lay still.

Rose looked at the old man in concern. "He must have run all the way, Tom. He looks exhausted." To Emily she said, "There's some water in the bucket out the back. Fetch this gentleman some water, if you please."

"Never mind the water," gasped the spinner. "Tom. You have to go to him. He's in a bad way."

Chapter 6

"**Y**ou're telling me you don't have the will to live anymore."

Mary slowly walked away from the bed, her body weak with despair, her eyes downcast. She pulled the curtains across the window, shutting out the blustery autumn day.

James lay propped up against the pillows, his eyes closed, his breathing shallow, and when he spoke, his voice was hoarse.

"Here, lass." His voice was soft and gentle as he reached for his wife's hand. "Don't talk like that, love. I've had a good life. A hard one, I'll grant you, but we have been happy, haven't we, Mary?"

Tom saw his mother's fear as spasms of violent coughing racked his father's weakened body, and he poured some water into a cup for her to give to him.

"Come on, love," she coaxed, holding it to his lips. "Try some. It'll cool your chest."

James took a sip but spluttered and he sank back onto the pillows, exhausted.

"We've been very happy, my love." Mary squeezed his hand. "I couldn't have wished for a better husband." She glanced at Tom, and then added cheerfully, "but you're going to get better, so we'll have no more talk like that."

"I won't get better, Mary. I've been ill for years, but I haven't always let on. But I'm worried about the business, lass. Can you and Tom keep it going?"

"You shouldn't have been outside in that damp shed so much. I swear that has something to do with it."

"It doesn't matter, lass. It had to be done."

Tom drew up a chair next to the bed so that he could speak to his father, who took his son's hands in his and held them tightly.

"We'll be fine. All of us. I've told you my plans, and I have every reason to think they'll work. I promise."

"But if you have to fight? How will your mother manage?"

"If I have to go I won't be away long. You'll continue with your spinning, won't you, mother?"

Mary nodded. Her face was wet with tears, and she brushed them away impatiently with the back of her hand. "This village looks after its own," she said, attempting a smile.

"You've seen Rose?" James was looking at him intently, and, ill as his father was, Tom knew that he couldn't lie to him.

"I've just come from there, but I don't know if I'll see her again. She's very protective of her little girl."

The spasm of coughing came again, and when it passed, James said. "Of course she is. Be persistent. Show her you care."

His mother looked at her son, her eyes pleading. "Leave us awhile, would you please love," she said quietly. "I want to sit with your father awhile."

Tom couldn't speak for the lump that was rising in his throat, and as he kissed his father's cheek he tried to convey in one intense gaze all the love and respect he had always felt for him. His eyes brimmed with tears as he fled from the room, leaving his parents together for the very last time.

To see his father in such a state had been a shock. That he had been able to talk to him, to reassure him that he would be able to cope, gave him slight comfort. He didn't want to watch him die, and he was grateful that his mother had excused him being there at the end.

He ran out of the house, his head down against the wind, without realising he was going in the direction of the little stream that ran along the bottom of the field by the ropeworks. He was so deep in misery that the frantic movement of the reeds seemed to mesmerise him as he approached the little wooden bridge, so that when he lost his balance he nearly tumbled into the water.

Shaken, he went to sit on the little wall that his father had built many years ago, making himself comfortable amongst the little pillows of mosses and lichen, their colours fading now with the onset of winter. He watched the mosquitoes chase each other under the aspen tree, at a point where the stream followed a curve and disappeared from view.

Tears blurred his vision, and he swallowed hard. He hadn't realised that losing a parent would hurt so much. When he had cried as a child, his mother had told him it was all right to show his feelings, even when he grew up, as it showed he cared. But it was better to do it alone, he decided. It was more dignified somehow.

Tom blamed himself for his father's ill health, and when he had looked down at him in his bed and seen the dullness in his eyes he realised that over the past few weeks he had aged ten years. He cursed himself for not having seen how the curve of his back had betrayed the symptoms of old age and depression, the wrinkles at the corners of his eyes that had recently deepened, and at his receding hairline only little tufts of grey remained where his hair had once grown thick and luxuriant. But his work hadn't suffered; perhaps that was the reason he hadn't noticed. Father would never have let them down with shoddy work, and he had worked until he had dropped, six days a week. At last he had settled into his chair, his day's work done, his fingers playing idly with a piece of twine, winding and rewinding it until it fell apart; it was as if he was afraid to abandon any aspect of his life's work.

His father had been so thrilled to have finished his bundles of cloth, so why had he taken him so lightly when all he needed was a little praise? He had pushed himself to the limit when all the time he must have been feeling terrible, determining not to allow his family to see his pain.

Tom looked down, distracted by a sudden movement below the surface of the water. He left the safety of the wall and went to sit on the bank, keeping his eyes fixed on the shadow as it moved downstream, and he watched it until it disappeared.

Impulsively he leaned forward and removed his shoes, throwing them onto the grass beside him. He put his feet into the water, thrusting them into the floating weed, feeling its tendrils running through his toes, and for a fleeting moment, just a moment, he felt calm.

He jumped as a vole plopped into the water beneath him and swam away, becoming hidden in a clump of weeds. The resulting splash interrupted his flow of thought, and after a while he became aware that he was not alone. His senses tingled, and he knew without a doubt that the silent figure standing above him was Rose. Her feet shuffled nervously in the muddy grass beside him, and as he looked up their eyes met, her gaze steady and unflinching, his startled and intrigued as he wondered why she had come.

"Will you join me?" He patted the grass invitingly, but she remained standing.

"It's too wet."

"Where's Emily?"

"I left her with my neighbour. I was worried about you." She paused, as if wondering what to say. "How's your father? " she said finally.

"I don't know, but I shouldn't think it'll be long now. Mother's with him."

There was a long silence, until Tom added, "she wanted to be on her own with him."

"I've not come to criticise, Tom." Rose laid her hand gently on his shoulder. "It's hard, losing someone, isn't it? I thought you might need some company, but if you'd rather be on your own…"

"No. I'm glad you've come." Her voice had been sympathetic, and Tom warmed to her. This woman was good for him, and he realised that if he wanted to talk to her he should at least be on the same level. He made an effort to stand, and she helped him to his feet.

The broad-chested sailmaker stood several inches taller than the woman who, although no classical beauty, possessed something he couldn't identify; it wasn't the heart shaped face framed by the mahogany curls, or the hazel eyes that seemed to follow his every move. It was something inside her that made her special, something that he did not want to share or live without, and he hoped Rebecca would understand. All he had to do now was to discover if Rose felt the same.

"Do you want to talk about him?" she asked softly.

Tom's eyes misted with tears, and for a moment he centred his thoughts on the man who had meant the world to him. "I want to remember him as he was, Rose. Oh, I shall go through the funeral and the burial, but I shall be thinking of his vitality, his enthusiasm, and all that he did for us. I owe him, Rose, and I'm going to make sure he gets his wish."

"It's important that the twine works keeps going then," Rose said bluntly. "Do you want me to help you?"

Tom took her face in his hands and kissed her firmly on the lips. "You're so trusting, Rose. You don't know me, or my past. Isn't there anything you want to ask?"

"You have a five year old boy. He must have had a mother once. You're not the kind to desert a woman. You'll tell me when you're ready."

"Rebecca was my life, and Ben's. She died a long time ago and I have to move on."

Rose slipped her hand into his. "Come on. Shouldn't we be getting back?"

The main street was full of dairy shorthorns on their way to milking, their swollen udders swinging beneath them, the mud squelching between their hooves. With practised ease the young couple squeezed through the endless stream of cows, dodging cowpats left in their wake, but no sooner had they left them behind than they narrowly avoided colliding with the squire's curricle, as it tore down the street, oblivious to the villagers going about their business.

"What's the hurry?" shouted Tom, as it continued up the hill towards Yeovil. "It's bad enough that we have to doff our caps to that man, let alone allow him to push us all around. It's time he learned a few lessons."

"Tell you what, Rose said thoughtfully. "I've heard he's renting out a few acres near the Manor House."

"Might be worth paying him a visit, d'you think?"

"I think it's worth a try."

"Right then. I'll do whatever it takes to save this business. I'll go and see him."

Mary was at her kitchen sink, her arms covered in grime, a tendril of grey hair hanging down over one eye, her face so full of distress that it made Tom want to cry. In a frenzy she started to wash the pots, banging them together, spilling water onto the floor so that she now stood in a pool of water. It was only when she removed the tendril with the back of her hand that he could see that his father's death had caused her eyes to sink into her lined, grey face, and her legs barely carried her to the breakfast table where she collapsed onto the wooden bench.

Tom was at her side in an instant, his arms wrapped around her, his face buried in her neck. For as long as they clung together their tears ran freely, Tom's whispered words of comfort calming her until gradually the tears died away, and the tension dissolved.

Rose stood by the window watching the private outpouring of grief, having no part in it, being merely an outsider looking in. Tom's mother hadn't noticed her arrival, and seemed oblivious of her presence, but it didn't matter. She felt no embarrassment, merely relief that mother and son had come together to express their sorrow and to find a way through it. She had no doubt that Tom would fulfil his responsibilities, and she resolved to help him as much as she could.

"Your father told me yesterday that he wanted to die in peace, and that his bones were to be buried in the churchyard where we were wed," Mary said softly. "Our wedding was such a happy day, Tom." Her voice died away, and it was almost as if she was speaking to herself. "Father was done out in a borrowed suit - real posh it were - and I wore a gown in watered silk with a straw hat tied up with cherry red silk ribbons."

"Oh, Tom. It were wonderful. " She looked up at him, and now Tom could see her eyes were bright with unshed tears. " We looked like the lord and lady of the manor. He knew how to behave like a gentleman, too He carried me on his arm everywhere. He once saw good things for us. Who would believe it would end like this?"

She walked over to the window and looked out into the street where children were playing in the mud, and as her tale unfolded, tears ran unchecked down Tom's cheeks.

"We were to have the best twine and flax works in the west of England, " she said, speaking softly. "Our children were to inherit the legacy to pass down through the generations, so whatever you say, Tom, all hope is gone now with this talk of industri sommat, I don't know what, and we ain't the only ones, Tom. Big hopes. Big ideas. All gone. Too big for our boots, we was. Been cut down to size now." She stopped speaking for a moment, as if she had forgotten what came next, but then she turned away from the window and stared at Tom, her eyes dark with despair, and when she spoke again her voice was heavy with emotion. "What have we done to deserve it, Tom? What have we done?"

Tom reached out for her, and she came to him again, weeping as if her heart would break. He spoke softly and stroked her hair until she quietened, giving out the love and support she so desperately needed.

"You haven't done anything wrong, mother," he whispered. "But nothing has been wasted, can't you see? Father has gone, and things will never be the same. We have to carry on, for his sake. He wouldn't have wanted you to give up. Our cloth has a good name, and we can make a good living from it."

Rose came away from the window and looked at Mary with a new understanding.

"We can do it, " she said, her eyes shining. "The whole world will know about Coker cloth. And when that Boney scuttles away down his little bolthole in France, we will have made some of the sails that lead the ships to victory. I'm willing to help, Mrs Welland. I know about sewing the seed, harvesting it, and the spinning. I've done it all my life. Won't you let me try?"

"You seem to have plenty of enthusiasm," Mary said tiredly. "I wish I could say the same for myself."

"You need a rest, mother," Tom said firmly. "Why don't you go and stay with your sister for a few days. It'll do you a world of good."

"I can't, not now. It isn't right. I have to stay and see to his things."

"There's no hurry. We can help you when you get back if you want."

"How will you manage the children?" Mary argued. "You can't run a business with young children running around."

"I think we need a change, too, mother. We could do with a holiday, and the children would love it, but besides speaking to the squire about renting some land I want to pay a visit to the spinning works in Bridport. I've been hearing good things about Gilbert's mill, and I think there's a lot we can learn from it."

"I didn't think you liked his methods," Mary retorted. "How will you live? Where will the money come from?"

"I don't know," Tom said honestly. "But it has to be done. I need to rethink a few things."

"But first we have a funeral to consider. I promised James he would be buried at St Martin's."

Mary seemed to have recovered her composure, and was making a brave attempt to take control of the situation. "So the sooner I go to see the vicar the better. James deserves the best we can afford."

Chapter 7

Clifford Sullivan was standing at his library window, looking out onto the windswept garden, deliberating over whether he had the energy to take a stroll around his vast acreage, or to take time to savour the contents of a cask of port wine sent to him the previous day by Lady Beamish from Dorchester.

He decided against the walk; he was too comfortable in his morning robe warming himself by his roaring fire, and besides, he was not in the best of tempers. His thoughts were busy with the memory of the hefty tax bill that had been sent to him by the government. How typical of that damned Pitt to perpetuate the property tax that was no doubt serving to meet the expenses of the French wars. He'd have to get rid of his newest carriage to meet that one, and that damned son of his didn't help, either; his taste for libidinous living had nearly bankrupted him over the past year. What he needed was a spell in the Navy, and a damned good flogging.

"To hell with them all," he growled, as he swept the offending papers from his desk, the warmth from the fire fuelling the burning resentment that threatened to burst from every pore of his bloated body.

The squire was seated at his heavy oak desk and didn't bother to look up when his visitor was ushered into the room.

But Tom, noting the droop of his shoulders, the heaviness of his eyelids, and an unpleasant scowl on his face, wished that he had chosen another day.

Slowly the squire raised his head and stared at him as if he were no better than one of his servants, and Tom stared back defiantly, refusing to be intimidated by this ignorant man who was flaunting his wealth by jangling the money in his pockets.

"And you are?"

"Tom Welland, sir. I run the ropeworks at the end of the village."

"Ah, yes." Clifford Sullivan leaned forward in his chair, rested his elbows on the desk and clasped his hands together. Suddenly he changed position, leaned back in his chair, laid his hands on his exceptionally corpulent stomach, and lifted his feet onto the desk. He contemplated his visitor through narrowed eyes.

"And what can I do for you?"

There was no offer of a chair so Tom remained standing. He watched in fascination as large drops of condensation ran down the squire's glistening forehead and settled on his bulbous nose. His face was turning an interesting shade of red, and Tom would have expected him to move away from the fire, but he was surprised by his reaction.

Seizing a lump of coal from the scuttle with a pair of tongs, the squire placed it on top of the burning heap, following it with several more lumps, and then, to ensure an instant blaze, pumped the bellows vigorously until the flames leapt even higher.

Tom tried to smother an impulsive smirk, but it proved an impossible task, and the squire pounced.

"Something is amusing you. Can we share the joke, Mr Welland?"

"Not at all, sir. I was merely stifling a sneeze."

"Well then, I suggest we get on with it."

Clifford Seymour resumed his position at his desk, and selected the fattest cigar from an exquisitely engraved wooden box. He lit it, inhaled, and settled back unhurriedly into his chair.

As a curl of blue smoke spiralled towards the ceiling, Tom thought he detected a hint of a smile. But what lay behind the smug exterior?

"What is it you require, Mr Welland?" The squire's tone had assumed its former sharpness.

Tom took a deep breath, "I would like to rent some of your land, sir, if that is possible."

"Presuming I have some to lease, eh?" The squire attempted a smile, but by drawing his lips back over chipped and uneven teeth managed only a kind of leer, and Tom took a step backwards.

"Running away, now, Mr Welland? Changed your mind?"

"Not at all," Tom said. "I believe you have some spare land and I wish to acquire it for a nominal sum."

"Straight to the point, eh?" Glad to see you have a bit of spirit, boy." The eyes narrowed again, the lips pursed and the fingers stubbed out the butt of his cigar, but Tom's reaction was measured, his features composed. He wasn't giving this man a chance to assert his control.

"I wish to grow some flax, sir, to supplement the amount I grow at the moment."

"Ah." The squire rubbed his hands together greedily.

Money meant power and respect, and Tom knew that if he gave him access to both the land was his for the taking.

"You're interested in becoming a Member of Parliament, I hear."

"Who told you that?"

"Oh come now, sir. As part of our respectable community I am privy to such information." Tom leaned over the desk and fixed him with a direct stare. "I can help you, you know. I might know the right sort of people to speak to. Important people."

"You're bluffing. You're only a small spinner."

Tom tapped his nose. "Oh, I know them all right. They're going to help me."

"Then they can give you the land. Ask them." The squire stood up, presuming the conversation to be at an end.

"They don't have land," Tom said, and then pushed home his advantage. "But they do have money, and power. And they know the Prime Minister."

"Who are they?" The squire sounded suspicious.

"You don't need to know, but I can tell you they are from the naval fraternity, and they have a lot of influence."

The fire had died down, and Clifford Seymour pumped it up again, throwing an extra lump of coal on top for good measure. He returned to his seat, rested his elbows on the table and leaned forward, his face merely inches from Toms, giving him the benefit of his foul breath.

The squire lit another cigar and puffed hard until it lit. "Deal with the Admiralty, do they?" he asked casually.

"Probably" Tom had the man eating out of his hand, and the land was about to become his. He was playing with him as a cat played with a mouse. Gullible fool!

"How will they help you?"

"All will be revealed in good time," Tom said mysteriously.

"Why should I trust you?"

"You can't. But I may be worth knowing in a few months."

The squire tried another approach. "You weave an excellent piece of cloth, I believe?"

"The best for miles around."

"Yet you don't have enough money for land. Are you sure you're not spinning me a tale, Mr Welland?"

"Maybe. You'll have to take that chance, I'm afraid," Tom said quietly. Greed would be this man's undoing, he thought with glee.

"All right. You can have ten acres. Two fields near Wash Lane. I'll get my solicitor to draw up the necessary papers. First payment on the first of the month. Don't let me down."

Rose greeted his news with approval. "I knew you could do it," she said happily. "Your father would have been proud of you."

They were in the ropewalk, laying out the skirders in rows along the length of the walk, horizontal bars that prevented the yarns from sagging on the ground, placing vertical pegs along them so that the yarns could be separated.

"He played right into my hands, Tom said, grinning. "When we come back from Bridport we're going to have a lot to do; extra machines, more labourers, and I wondered whether it would be worth trying Russian seed. I hear it's all the rage in West Dorset. It makes excellent cloth, I understand." He paused, and a frown puckered his brow.

"What is it Tom? There's nothing wrong, is there?" Rose came towards him, walking between the skirders.

Tom looked down at her and smiled. "No, Rose. Nothing's wrong. I don't like to let a child down, that's all. I made Emily a promise, and I think it's important to keep it."

Rose looked puzzled. "I don't remember you making her a promise." Then she smiled. "Unless you mean that business with the candle."

"I think we should have an outing to Yeovil to buy a candle mould from the tallow chandler," Tom said. "It's Friday tomorrow, and I've some raw flax that might fetch a few pennies. Enough to buy Emily a new pair of shoes, perhaps."

"You don't want to be spending your money on my daughter, Tom. Your mother needs looking after."

"I should like Emily to have some shoes. I think she deserves to have comfortable feet."

"If you're sure…it's very kind of you."

"I'm sure."

Tom took her hand and together they walked back to the cottage, where Ben and Emily were being looked after by one of Rose's friends.

"You're very quiet, Rose," Tom commented, looking at her in concern. "You haven't said much since we left the field. What's the matter?"

"I don't think you have a lot of money," Rose said softly. "And I can't let you waste it on me, or Emily. You have to save what little you have."

"To hell with money," Tom said impatiently. "Money is nothing unless you can help the ones you love. I need to go to market anyway, and a tallow mould won't break the bank. Let me do the worrying."

But in reality he was worried. There would be competition to supply the best cloth to the Navy, and there was no guarantee that he would be successful. He hadn't been able to convince his mother either. But he had to try. People's lives depended on it. In frustration he beat his clenched fist into his open palm, startling her.

"Look, Tom," she said gently. "Let me help you, please. Let's take it a step at a time. We'll go to the market, buy what we need, and then we can sit down and talk about what to do next. You don't have to carry all this on your shoulders, you know."

Ben came in from the garden, closely followed by Emily, and as soon as he saw his father he leapt on him with a shriek of delight.

"See, Emily, I told you daddy wouldn't be long," he said, flashing his father a mischievous grin. "You said we could go to the market. Can we? Oh please say we can."

"Have you been good?" Tom ruffled his hair.

"I didn't mean to hurt Henry," Ben admitted. "I trod on his tail and sat on him. But he didn't meow. I don't think he minded."

"And Emily, have you been good, or have you been tormenting Nancy?" Rose surveyed the muddy feet and scraped knees in mock horror and her daughter giggled.

"We washed Henry under the pump, mummy, and now he's nice and clean, look."

Rose exchanged glances with her friend and they both sighed. The bedraggled cat was languishing on the windowsill outside, and Tom let it in. With a screech it fixed its claws onto his leg, then darted up the stairs and hid under a bed.

Pain made him cry out in anger, and afraid he would punish them by forbidding their treat, the children were contrite and pleaded with him, while Rose cleaned the wound and wrapped it in a clean cloth.

"If you want to go to Yeovil morrow we'll have to find someone who will lend us a wagon." Rose winked at Tom as she tied a knot in the bandage and helped him onto a chair so that he could rest his leg. "Do you think you'll be well enough to go, Tom?" Rose winked at him.

"It depends if Abe Freeman has a mare." He paused, as if considering the situation, then added, "I don't suppose there's any point until we see if I can walk. Rose. Will you help me up from the chair to see if I can put my foot on the floor?"

He pretended to stumble and clutched the leg of the table for support. He looked at the children's faces, and frowned. "Oh dear, it doesn't look too good, does it? What are we going to do?"

"You're telling us fibs," shouted the children. "Your leg isn't really hurt."

"Don't you think so?"

"No we don't."

"What do you think, Emily's mum?"

"I think you should try again. It might be mended now." Rose grinned.

Tom stood up and chased the children out of the room, and he could hear them laughing as they ran upstairs.

He took her arm as they walked back to the kitchen. "We get on rather well as a family, don't you think, Rose? The children seem to like each other, too. We ought to have more outings. What d'you say to buying our own wagon when we can afford it?"

Rose blushed and moved away from him. "I need to speak to you about 'us,' Tom, she said quietly. "I've said I'll help you but things are going too quickly. I like you a lot, and I enjoy doing things with you. You have explained about your wife, and I value that. You also know my position." She took a deep breath. "But I don't know how much...what I mean to say is...how much..."

Tom tilted her chin with his finger and kissed her tenderly. "There," he said softly. "How much do you think I like you now?"

Rose smiled. "I should think you like me as much as I like you, Mr Welland. And I should like to get to know you even better, if you'll let me."

"That's exactly what I do want, Mrs Howard. To be quite honest, after Rebecca died I never thought I could love again, but emotion is a strange feeling. One minute you believe that you will keep the memory of your adored wife alive in your heart forever, with no room for anyone else, and the next you meet someone you can't bear to be without. "

"Love at first sight, you mean?"

"I think that's what it must be, Rose. I hope we have a future, and I want you to be with me whenever you can. So, will you and Emily come to the market tomorrow?

Rose grinned. "I certainly will," she said.

"I've never been to Yeovil afore," Emily said, as she and Ben jumped up and down in the cart as they drove towards the town, making it sway as they passed by Hendford House, its iron railings protecting its ivy clad hamstone walls.

"Sit down or you'll fall out," Rose ordered as they rounded the corner by the post office at the top of the High Street. The children stared open mouthed as a stagecoach passed through the arched entrance of the Mermaid Inn, sweating horses in front, luggage on top, the guard about to jump down onto the straw strewn yard.

Tom pulled up in the Borough, and tethered the mare to the one remaining pillar at the Market House. Chaos surrounded them; people mingled with horse-drawn wagons, carts displayed goods, there were standings with open baskets, block trestles, hampers, animals and poultry of all kinds. There was little room to move, and at first Tom and Rose carried the children on their shoulders in case they lost them.

"Look over there, Emily," cried Ben. "There's that lady from East Coker. I want to get down."

"Don't go too far," Tom warned the children, immediately regretting his decision as they slipped through the crowded market place in a bid to greet Aunty Bess. In an instant they were absorbed into the throng of people milling about the Borough. Bess was so engrossed in making a good deal with the purveyor of two oxen that she was unaware of either the family's existence, or the dilemma the children's disappearance had caused.

The market closed around them as Tom and Rose began searching for their children, frantically calling their names, looking inside wagons, cattle pens, shops and the straw in the well-named Shambles.

Ben and Emily were enjoying themselves, rummaging through a basket of knick knacks, casting boxes of buttons, ribbons and lace to the four winds, unaware that their parents were desperately looking for them.

"Oi! Look what you're doing, ye young devils," shouted the possessor of the merchandise. "Where's yer father? What you two need is a good wallopin'." The red faced fellow sighed, put down his mug of cider, heaved his bulk out of his seat and attempted to chase Ben and Emily down the road. He reached the corner of Grope Street before giving up, bent double with a searing pain in his side, grunting in annoyance as the children ran off laughing along Middle Street.

The large bellied basket holder now claimed the attention of nearby traders, explaining in detail how he had been robbed. And Tom, having at last grasped the fact that Emily and Ben were about to be accused of stealing, thrust some coins into the man's hand and chased after them.

He sprinted through the narrow street full of irregularly built houses, casting anxious glances around him in the hope of finding his children. He tripped over a loose stone and sprawled headlong across the pavement, but he picked himself up and carried on. He reached the George Inn, and there they were, sitting on top of a low stone wall, dangling their legs, waiting for him.

"What the hell do you think you are doing," he shouted. "You stupid children. Don't you know that you can be hanged for stealing?"

"I didn't rob him," protested Ben. "We was looking for a present for Emily's mum. Don't be silly, father. If we're found guilty we won't be hanged. We'll have to spend time in the stocks, and I don't care. It was worth it. "

Tom lifted his son down from his perch and smacked him hard on the leg. Ben started to howl, frightening Emily, who joined in.

"I'm not sorry I did that," Tom said angrily. "I am not being silly, and if you ever call me that again you'll be in for an even bigger hiding."

"We didn't steal anything, honest we didn't, dad."

"That naughty man was lying, Mr Welland," said Emily, between loud sniffs. She held out her hands, spreading her fingers wide. "Look. We've got nuffin.' We can't be hanged 'cos we've got nuffin.'"

"Why did you run away, then, eh?"

"We thought it was fu…".

Ben kicked her, and she screwed up her face in pain. But it had stopped her from admitting that she had at first thought the situation funny, risking greater punishment.

He grabbed them both by the arm and marched them down the road

"Where are we going dad? I thought we were looking for a candle mould," protested Ben.

"You can forget the mould," Tom said angrily. "I need to get you away from here. Have you seen that group of traders coming towards us?"

"It's too late," said Ben. They'll be here in a minute."

For a moment they stood uncertainly, unsure which way to run, or whether to run at all, and anyway, what would be the point? They were hemmed in from all directions, as traders were entering the other end of the street from Vennell's Cross, and it wouldn't be long before they were caught in the middle.

Suddenly Rose appeared from one of the side roads, having taken a different route, and after realising the trouble they were in, she ran towards her daughter and wrapped her arms around her to keep her safe.

Anxiously she looked down into Emily's tear stained face and with a finger drew aside her bedraggled fringe, wet with perspiration.

"Are you all right?" she asked, her voice shaking.

Emily nodded.

"You're going to have to be brave, you know."

Emily nodded again and clung to her mother in fear.

"There they are!"

Bravely Tom walked forward and faced them; Rose took the children behind the wall of the Inn and they crouched down behind it.

"Hand them over," demanded the basket stallholder, standing with his feet astride, so that his bulk was evenly distributed. His muscles hardened beneath his shirt, and Tom, being of medium build and several inches shorter, realised his chances were not good, not good at all.

"I want to see those little thieves punished. Let me at them."

"Prove that they have stolen from you." Tom's voice was strong and clear. " I've paid you, so let that be an end to it."

"Ha!" The brute lurched towards him, his tongue flicking over his thick lips, and he drew them back to reveal several blackened teeth, his breath so foul that it made Tom want to retch. "I fancy the thought of ripping off the other ear. Care to stop me?" he threatened.

Tom paled, and the brute pounced.

"You realise that by giving me money you are admitting your guilt," said the bully. "Lead me to a magistrate, brothers. Let's see them punished. They won't be robbing no-one else if I have anything to do with it."

"I paid you out of good faith," Tom protested. "I know they had nothing on them because I searched them myself."

The basket holder laughed out loud. "You are a joke, sir. Do you really expect me to believe that? Well, perhaps you would prefer to fight for your honour, and when your children see you lying bloody in the street, they will know what their actions have caused."

"Whatever good will fighting do?" Tom said quietly. "Can't you see how frightened they are?"

"And so they should be," the bully said smugly. "Someone needs to be taught a lesson, and it might as well as well be you." In a flash he had drawn back his arm and punched Tom on the nose, and Rose watched him fall to the pavement with a thud.

The scuffle had been watched by a man who had every reason to be interested in their progress, and especially the lady, whom he had never seen before. Clifford Seymour was sitting near a window inside the George, where he had been for the last two hours drinking ale. Now he rolled out of the door and into the street, staggering towards the man lying on the ground.

"You seem to have got yourself into a bit of trouble, haven't you?" The squire prodded Tom with his foot.

"Get up."

Tom held out his hand and the squire tried to help him up, but he lost his balance and joined Tom on the pavement.

Tom scrambled to his feet and looked down at the man on the ground in contempt. "You may think yourself a country squire, but you are certainly no gentleman." He grinned. "Perhaps I should walk away and let your friends pick you up."

"I wouldn't advise it, Welland. I believe you asked me for a little favour the other day?"

The admission was pounced upon by the basket holder. "What favour was that, Welland?"

"None of your business," Tom snapped.

With difficulty the squire stood up, and then he belched. "Mr Welland here wants to rent my land. Tell him why that is, sir, or would you rather introduce me to that gorgeous creature of yours?" Seymour's appreciative gaze took in Rose's slim waist and shapely ankles, and when he winked at her she turned away in embarrassment.

"I wouldn't mind a bit of that myself." Slowly he walked towards Rose and tickled her under the chin with his middle finger.

Tom was seething with anger, and he raised his fist to strike him, but aware that he was taking centre stage, his audience judging his every move, he thought better of it and his arm fell uselessly to his side.

"Why should I want to fight with you? Have a little respect for yourself."

"Wise man." The squire chuckled, an unpleasant gurgling sound made deep in his throat, and Rose drew Emily even closer.

"I think you should go back inside," Tom said. "You aren't serving any purpose out here."

"On the contrary, I have plenty to say. I may be drunk, but I know what I am talking about. I think we should return to the subject of my land. Tell these people how you tried to bribe me."

Tom said nothing.

"Well, if you won't, I will." Clifford Seymour raised his voice to speak to the traders. "Thomas Welland here said he had lot of influence with important people who could help me become a Member of Parliament. Put in a good word for me, he said. Well, I'm afraid I don't believe you. You've cheated me, sir, and I'd rather not rent you my land. I'm sure there are farmers amongst you who would intensively cultivate it to give me better profits, without resorting to bribery. Someone who would be a sub-tenant, perhaps."

"If you don't want my help, that's fine with me," said Tom. "I'll manage."

"I own land for miles around," the squire said spitefully.

"I said, I'll manage. Now. If that's all you have to say…"

"You want to get your hands on my land because you want to expand your sailcloth business, never mind the needs of your neighbours. And as flax around here makes exceedingly good cloth I think there would be many interested parties. So. How about it, gentlemen?"

Chapter 8

Bess was furious. Several days later she summoned Tom and made it clear that she was disappointed in him.

"There is a rumour going around the village that you have had an unpleasant meeting with Squire Seymour. Am I right?"

Tom nodded. "I'm afraid so, Bess. The circumstances were not what I would have wished."

Tom knew when Bess was mad with him. Her eyes flashed and her cheeks reddened until she lost her temper. It was a frightening experience and he gritted his teeth.

"Obviously you know that you have alienated the traders in the town at a time when you need their support, and it serves you right. You knew our arrangement was supposed to be a secret, Tom, so how could you use it to make a deal with a man like that? I could have found some land for you to rent if only you'd asked. Now the whole town will know and although you may think its no big thing it's important to me. I wanted you to do well, Tom. Your mother and I have been friends for years. She and your father loved each other so much, and they didn't have an easy life, you know. Your father wanted to leave you something worthwhile, and I know that when he died he thought he'd failed you. So I was pleased that you had the enthusiasm to want to make something of yourself, and improve the business, and I had thought I could help you with your accounts; your mother doesn't have time to show you." Suddenly her voice softened. "Now...I don't know. It depends whether I can placate them. I can try, but I don't know if they will listen to an old woman like me. Tell me; how is your mother"

"She's temporarily staying with relatives."

"She'll come back, of course."

"I'm sure she will, when she feels better. She was pretty upset, you know."

"I can imagine." Bess hesitated and her fingers played with the lace edging on her shawl. "She is aware of your…er…new friend, is she?"

"Rose? Of course."

"She lives with you?"

Suddenly Tom felt angry, very angry. How dare this woman suggest that he and Rose were living together?

"Mrs Howard lives in her cottage with her daughter," he snapped. "Emily and Ben are good friends. It's good for single children to play together. But what has it to do with you? I am an adult, and so is Rose, and we are old enough to live our lives as we wish. And that's all I'm going to say on the matter. Can't you trust me to do the right thing?"

"Do you love her?"

"Although it's none of your business, as a matter of fact I do, and yes, I know what I said after Rebecca, but these things happen. Anyway, mother likes her so that's all that matters."

"I am pleased to hear it."

Tom sighed and sat down heavily in a chair. "Bess. There's room for all of us in this business. And you know I value your advice, don't you?"

Bess nodded, but her expression showed otherwise.

"Mother will soon be home and then you'll be able to see for yourself that things are working out. I'll take care of her, I promise. She may be fragile for a while, but I want to show her that life can still be worth living and that she can be happy. I love her too, you know."

Oh, what the hell! He thought. Why was he trying so hard? Bess would see what she wanted to see. He wouldn't be asking her for help with the land. He and Rose would show her that they could manage on their own.

It was late spring when Tom decided to take Rose to Bridport, and he thought it better to leave the children behind with Rose's friend Nancy, if she would have them.

It was part of his plan to visit the town by the sea, where the light, well-drained soil was ideal for growing flax and hemp. His true interest lay in the warehouses that lay near the harbour and the ships that would eventually take his exports all over the world. The previous day he had received permission from the owner of the mill at Burton Bradstock to inspect his products with a view to doing business with him, and that was the official reason for his visit.

The village of Burton Bradstock lay east of the mouth of the river Bride, which drove the mills that turned out not only ropes and sails but cloth bags, tarpaulin sheeting and hammocks. As well as the handloom weavers and spinners that were employed within the mills, weaving was carried out by outworkers, another idea that he wanted to explore. The visit would take at least two days and he intended to raid his savings box kept for special occasions such as this. He needed to spend a little if he wanted to make the most of business opportunities. But first he needed to talk to his workers to ensure that they would be happy to work without them, as the rope works would need to run at full capacity, or there would be no business for them to manage on their return.

Tom and Rose travelled through East Coker, and then took the road to Corscombe. The lanes were crooked but narrow and full of muddy dips and hollows, but Emma was sure-footed until they started to climb the steep road leading to Beaminster Down, when she started to tire. Taking pity on her, Tom unhitched the cart and allowed the panting animal to cool down by a little brook.

Rose stretched her legs as she wandered through the sparse furze, letting the wind blow through her hair. The panoramic view below was breathtaking; the verdant hues of the forest of trees converged, allowing a flash of the blue waters of the bay to peep through. And where winter had taken its toll of the stubble fields, freshly planted corn now showed brown under the pale sun. Distant villages were hidden from view within the folds of the coombes and spinneys; not far away was the village of Netherbury, the home of the Hood family.

"I've never seen anything so beautiful," she whispered.

"You should see it in the autumn. It's even lovelier then."

"How far away is the sea?" Rose cuddled up to him, and he slid an arm about her waist. The sweet smell of her made him unable to resist pulling back the hood of her cloak and kissing her.

He could feel her tremble at his touch; he was finding it difficult to hold back, and knew that it would not be long before he took her to his bed and showed her how much he loved her. But it was too soon for them both. He had to be sure her troubles from the past had been resolved before he burdened her with his own.

"A few miles yet," he said at last.

He was finding it hard to control the tremor in his voice, yet there was so much he wanted to say. Instead of speaking words of love, he described the journey that lay ahead of them; the splendours of the Dorset coast that never failed to inspire him, and his love of the people who laboured in the mills in the winter, but escaped to their seine boats during the fishing season when they could make a few extra shillings to spend on ale and cider.

"Have you seen the sea before?" he asked softly.

Rose shook her head.

"Let me paint you a picture." His arm swept the landscape from left to right as he described the scene.

"Imagine enchanting coves and harbours that nestle below high cliffs all along the Dorset coast. The river Bride flows from the hills and down into the sea south of Burton Bradstock at Burton Freshwater, where the flax is dew retted and spread out to weather in the sun. The pebbles there are as small as peas, but when you get to Portland at the other end of Chesil Beach, the pebbles are the size of saucers.

"Why's that then, Tom?"

"Apparently it's something to do with the movement of the waves, but I'm not sure," Tom admitted. "Nature's a strange thing."

"What happens to the sails and nets that are made at Bridport? Do they have a carrier service like we do?"

"I think so. Yes, of course they do. But goods not sent by ship go by chaise mail coach from the Greyhound Inn in East Street. Ropes and nets are exported from the harbour at Bridport to places in Europe, Africa and North America, so there's no reason why we can't send our cloth overseas, too. While we're here I want to look at the warehouses to find out whether I can store our goods there until a ship collects them."

Tom helped Rose into the cart and took the reins, moving off down the hill towards Beaminster. She pulled up the hood of her cloak to protect her from the crisp cold air that stung their faces, turning their cheeks red.

Even before the sea came into view Tom tasted the familiar saltiness of it on his tongue, and a thrill ran through him at the thought of spending time alone with Rose in one of the prettiest places in England.

They drove on for a while enjoying the scenery, until Rose broke the silence.

"Emily wants to know where sailcloth was first made in England, Tom, and in which century. I told her you would know."

Tom looked at her and smiled. "Thanks to my father I do. He reckoned that in the middle of the seventeenth century the King of France wouldn't allow anyone in his country to export it, and at the end of that century the people of Somerset started to make it. Then people living in Bristol and Dorchester became interested. In fact, in seventeen forty-six no British built ship was allowed out of port unless her first suit of sails were entirely British."

They had reached the tollgate at Clampits, on the road between Netherbury and Beaminster. Tom paid his dues, and continued on his way, but a road wagon was lumbering along in front of them, and it wasn't long before he lost both his temper and his patience.

"Get that damned thing of the road," he shouted. "A snail could travel faster than you."

"I pays me tolls, the same as you," yelled the driver, and continued his leisurely pace, his wagon piled dangerously high with goods, which had slipped to one side and were threatening to fall off.

"Silly fool." Tom assumed a pious expression, and urged Emma into a trot, determined to beat the driver in front, with no thought for either his mare or his passenger.

"Tom!" Rose screamed at him at she clung on to the side of the cart, bracing herself for a collision, and gasped with relief as they slithered to a stop a few yards behind the wagon, her hat hanging around her neck by its ribbon.

"What the hell was all that about?" she snapped. "You're lucky nothing from that wagon fell on me. I want to get out." She stood up, preparing to climb out, but Tom pulled her back.

"I'm sorry. I shouldn't have done that." He tried to put his arms around her, but she pushed him away, and as he slumped back into the driving seat he knew that she had seen the kind of behaviour that she would never tolerate again. Ever.

They continued the rest of the journey in silence, with Tom trying to think of a way to show her how sorry he was, and that she could trust him.

At lunchtime they stopped at the White Heart in Hogshill Street, the main coaching inn and meeting place in Beaminster, but Rose hesitated before entering the dining room.

"Aren't you hungry?" Tom sounded concerned.

Rose shook her head.

Lamplight bathed the room in a warm glow, making it look cosy, bringing relief from the cold weather outside, but Rose preferred to linger in the doorway, unwilling to follow him to a seat by the fire.

"Please, Rose. You need to eat. You look cold. Come and get warm and I'll order something for you."

Again Rose shook her head, and Tom, determined to be friends with her, tried again.

"Please, my love," he said softly. "I'm sorry. I was stupid and I've learned my lesson. I have a temper and I must learn to control it. Will you help me do that, please?"

And then she smiled, and to Tom it seemed as if the sun had come out again.

"I'd like some fish," she said. "Some mackerel perhaps. It depends what they have."

"And a slice of bread and butter."

She smiled, and Tom knew that he was truly forgiven. Happily he went to order the meal, knowing that everything would be all right.

"The thing is," Rose said when he returned, "I was angry because I was thinking that if we had been driving with Emily or Ben in the cart, they could have fallen out and been trampled on." She saw him frown, but continued, "I needed to say that Tom, because it is important."

She unfolded her napkin and laid it on her lap. "I needed to say that, and now I shall say no more about it and enjoy my meal."

When they came out of the inn it was raining, and tenderly Tom pulled Rose's cloak more firmly around her and climbed into the driving seat.

Tom kept his head down with his coat collar turned up against the rain. He was pleased that Emma was lively and he spurred her on, anxious for a change of clothing, and the pair of them were relieved when they reached Burton Bradstock.

Emma trotted on through Church Street, where the cottages clustered unevenly along the road, their thatched roofs sweeping low over dormer windows and limestone walls, but when they reached the busy thoroughfare to the mill they found it blocked with flax carts.

Tom tensed; his heart was beating with excitement, yet he was tormented by feelings of uncertainty. Was he doing the right thing, paying a visit to a business rival to discover the reason for his prosperity, whilst inventing another reason for his visit? That he was not morally right and that his father would have been disappointed in him was of great concern to him, and that he had involved the woman he loved in this deception could be viewed as behaving badly, to say the least. But in his defence he considered that he needed to learn from those who had proved themselves in the sail making business, so that he could use the knowledge gained for the benefit of others.

He glanced at Rose, who was biting her lip in concentration as she steered the cart around the scattered employees' houses, yet again feeling pride in her many talents, whilst being humbled by her loyalty. He had been surprised at her determination to accompany him, but at the same time delighted that she had showed an interest in his

business, and that she understood so well everything he was trying to accomplish. She was an extraordinary woman.

They clattered around the millpond and past the warehouses and offices, finally reaching the thatched stone house at the end of the lane.

A middle-aged woman left the open doorway and came to meet them, her cashmere shawl drawn tightly about her shoulders. Her pale hair had been cut close to her head in a feathered style and she was wearing an Indian muslin in a warm pink and brown shade, a perfect match for her buckled pale pink shoes. She held out her hand.

"Mr Welland. Lovely to see you. Come inside out of the rain, and let me take your cloak, Mrs Welland."

"We're not married," Rose said firmly. "But you can call me Rose if you like. I am Mr Welland's business companion. "

"Ah."

That single word conveyed a whole world of understanding to Rose, and she frowned. She guessed what Margaret Gilbert thought of her, but she didn't care, She was no better than her; more money perhaps, but no better. And she would prove it.

Mrs Gilbert hung Rose's cloak on a hook behind the door whilst Tom was handing Emma and the cart to one of the workers, and then they both followed the lady of the house into the comfortably furnished parlour.

"Perhaps you would care for a cup of tea and a slice of home made cake, and a chance to dry out in front of the fire? I'm afraid my husband is late for his lunch. He took on another apprentice today. It takes a while to settle them in."

Tom felt uncomfortable and moved to the doorway. "We're taking up your time, Mrs Gilbert, Perhaps…"

"I'm sure he'll be home in a moment. Sit yourselves down. The kettle is coming to the boil."

The pastel colours of the furnishings in the room were beautifully toned, the large windows so positioned that the room caught the morning sun. Family portraits adorned the walls; the largest depicting a refined elderly gentleman with an intelligent face hung above the heavily mantled fireplace, in front of which stood a hand worked fire screen covered with roses.

"Did you have a good journey?" enquired Mrs Gilbert, as she re-entered the room carrying a tray full of cups and saucers. She laid them down on a small table and started to pour the milk. "I understand that you run a small twine works, Mr Welland." Suddenly she laid down the jug and looked at him. "I am curious to know why do you wish speak to my husband? He is a very busy man, you know. That 's why he insists on an appointment."

"Yes. And I'm grateful for his time, Mrs Gilbert." He hesitated. This woman was being so accommodating; perhaps it was time to tell the truth, and to hell with the consequences.

"I think your husband's achievements are outstanding, Mrs Gilbert. He is what a dear friend of mine would call an entrepreneur, not afraid to take responsibility for trying something new. I want to be like him, and I wondered if he would be so kind as to pass on some of the secrets of his success."

For a moment there was an ominous silence, until Mrs Gilbert spoke.

"Well, I am flattered, Mr Welland. But I'm a little confused. Why should my husband want to pass on his secrets? I should have thought he'd be better to keep them to himself, so if everyone were to share them he would not be as successful, do you not think?"

"Normally, yes. But we are about to enter a war that could prove to be a disaster for our country. I think we should all work together for the good of our people, doing what we do best, and that is to supply sails and products for the Navy. Don't you agree, Mrs Gilbert?"

"Mr Welland. My husband is proud of his achievements, and I don't know how he would react to your idea. I can see your point, but will he?" Margaret Gilbert spoke with her hands, moving her fingers elegantly to support her argument. She was the sort of woman, Tom thought, who was used to getting her own way, and doubtless the power behind her husband. And then he had a flash of intuition. This is how Rose would behave, he thought. But he would never allow her to influence his every thought and deed.

He tried to rid himself of his concerns and concentrate on the task in hand.

It would seem that it was this woman he must impress before he even met her spouse.

"I don't think it's important who provides what for the Navy as long as it is provided," he said passionately. "Surely, if we all work together and pool our resources and our time we will accomplish so much more."

"But why my husband's business, Mr Welland? Don't you know anyone closer to home you could motivate?"

"Of course." Tom's mind was whirling. Why had he not thought of it before? Why not make some kind of alliance in the southwest? There were plenty of people nearer to home than Jim Gilbert. Many of Yeovil's surrounding towns could be included, and the more he thought about the plan the more he warmed to it and realised that it was possible.

"Your husband must have a wealth of experience, Mrs Gilbert," Tom said, trying to be tactful. "He also has a large factory and access to a harbour to distribute his goods. I have a few contacts, a small amount of land, and a team of willing labourers. What would you say if I suggested that we combine businesses, for the purpose of the war, at least, then afterwards…"

"Who wants to combine businesses?"

The voice was deep and vibrant, and seconds later a well-built man walked into the room carrying a small case. He towered over Tom, who began to wither under his intense gaze whilst he waited for the factory owner's judgment of his untimely suggestion.

Jim Gilbert's bushy eyebrows were raised in anticipation, and Tom sought desperately for a way out of his dilemma. He would have preferred to have explained his reasons before being judged on his intentions, but it was too late. He was being forced to explain to one of the most powerful factory owners in the southwest why he considered merging several businesses on the basis of a war that not everyone was convinced would happen.

"I don't mean actually combine. I - I meant, couldn't we all work together for the same cause?"

"Don't we do that already, Mr Welland?"

"In a way. But there are many things I still need to learn."

"You mean, you want to steal my ideas and pass them off as your own."

"No, I didn't mean that at all," Tom said firmly. "I want to help all the small businesses in my area … and yours too, of course," he added hastily. "But machines are taking the place of the workers, and the larger mills and industries will take away our living if we don't keep up with progress."

"I don't see how I can help you," said the mill owner. "I live some way from you, and I am satisfied with the way I operate. I cannot help with the provision of machinery. I have enough for my own needs, and trust you will acquire your own in tome."

"Until village labourers can afford to pay for this machinery they have to compete against businessmen such as yourself, or many of them will lose their jobs," Rose said furiously, who until now had been standing quietly listening to the animated conversation, her hands balling into fists as she became more and more annoyed. "There are new economic opportunities coming, and I believe we can market the goods we produce by collectively sending them via the same carrier, and exporting them by sea to reach various destinations over and above the ones we regularly use. If we don't make a place for ourselves in the world we will be left behind."

Tom flashed her a grateful look, but Jim Gilbert hadn't finished.

"I do not appear rude, Mrs er…"

"My name is Rose. Rose Howard."

"All right, Rose. Do you know the difficulties involved in running a large mill; renewing and repairing the machinery, controlling insolent children, making sure that everyone is paid and that rules of safety are observed? You cannot know of any of these things when everything you do is run on a much smaller scale. I cannot teach you, it is something you learn over time, and time is something you do not have."

"With respect, Mr Gilbert, that is where you're wrong," Rose said sharply, high colour rushing to her cheeks, her eyes glittering like shards of grey ice.

"Who better than one of the little people to understand the needs of the labourers who do not know what it is like to have a decent night's sleep, little or no time to feed themselves, sacked if they are not quick enough about their work, their meagre wages given to their parents to feed their families?" She paused for breath. "What chance do they have to play in the open air, to have fun, as no doubt you did during your own childhood?"

Tom froze. Whatever was the matter with her? Was she paying him back for his bad behaviour, and did she not realise that she had probably finished his career? Rose might feel strongly about pauperised families, but now was not the time to air her opinion. He glanced at Mrs Gilbert, whose mouth had fallen open in shock. It looked as if he had reached the end of the road.

Chapter 9

"With respect, Rose," Jim Gilbert said sharply. "I hope you are not describing the people who work in my mill."

"Oh, but I am," cried Rose passionately. "Those little ones should be playing outside, not running around under dangerous machines."

"Have you seen my children? No? Then perhaps you should, and then you will see for yourself they are not the poor little things you think they are," Jim Gilbert said angrily. "Do you know, for instance, that when the fishing season comes along, off they go with their parents to make extra money from the mackerel they catch, and I have to wait until they come back. Of course, Mrs Howard, you don't live near the sea, so a season's fishing is unlikely to affect you."

Rose had been humiliated, but during the awkward silence that followed, she had time to think, and now realised that perhaps she should keep her dignity at all costs. She held out her hand.

"I'm sorry, Mr Gilbert. I didn't realise. Tom says my maternal instincts would get me into trouble one day. I hope there are no hard feelings?"

"It seems you have many things to learn about our trade, Mrs Howard. However, I believe your reasons to be altruistic, and to show you I am not the penny-pinching businessman you think I am, I am prepared to allow you to look around our spinning mill," he said, walking over to the window and looking out at the bleak wintry weather. As he closed it, he added, "no doubt you will find quite a difference in our methods, but my foreman will show you around, and then you can see for yourselves that I don't mistreat my employees. Tomorrow we can talk business, and see how I can help with warehouse space, and perhaps the odd boat or two. Now then, my dear," he said, looking at his wife. "How about another pot of tea? And I would imagine Tom and Rose would like to stay for the night, so perhaps you could organise a couple of rooms."

"That is very kind of you," Tom said. "May I say that Rose and I appreciate your generosity, especially after we have been less than civil. Is there any way that we can repay you?"

"That will not be necessary, Tom - is it all right for me to call you by your Christian name?"

"Of course."

"I'll admit that you have shamed me. I have been so busy making money that I have overlooked one vital thing, the welfare of my workers. I think you are both very brave in your endeavours, and I would like to address my shortcomings. Maybe you will be kind enough to answer some of the questions that have recently occurred to me about your own business. But before that, would you both care to join us by taking a glass of port?"

So, until they retired to bed, Tom and Rose told their story of the Coker Ropeworks; how Tom's mother and father, with very little capital had set up the business, and after his father's death their determination to improve the rope works.

"We couldn't manage without mother now," Tom explained. "At first, she suffered a period of mourning, but now she works with us; in fact, there's very little that she cannot do."

"There's one thing that puzzles me," said Jim Gilbert. "How is that you can afford to spend time away from your business? Surely you have not left your mother on her own?"

"Of course not. Our small labour force can be trusted to work well in our absence, and when we return we hope to be able to set up a new workroom so that we can employ more people."

"So that's where I come in. I understand what you are trying to accomplish, and it is commendable," said Jim Gilbert. "But it will be a tough journey for you both. I hope the little help I can give will prove to be of worth."

"Does Jim Gilbert make any other goods?" Rose asked conversationally as they trotted along Mill Street the following morning.

The sun had replaced the dark clouds from the day before and many of the doors of the cottages were standing open. Women sat in their doorways wearing bonnets and colourful scarves and aprons as they braided nets, the smaller children helping to thread the wooden needles from the hank of twine stretched over the Bridport Cross, whilst in the alley ways and back gardens the husbands and sons made twine. These were the outworkers who added to the labour force, and, Tom realised now, that he would have to add to those he already employed to man the new ropewalk he would build to turn out the sails.

"I think he manufactures tarpaulin sheeting, which is used on ships and by farmers," he said. "Then there are hammocks, tablecloths, napkins and towelling, and he's always looking for new ideas."

"You were lucky he forgave you," said Tom. "That grovelling was a bit excessive."

"I had to do something," Rose admitted. "I knew you wouldn't be happy if you didn't get a look at that mill."

As Tom adjusted his eyes to the gloom, a steady roar, deep and persistent, filled his whole being, and above this, too, was the penetrating hum of belts and running wheels. They climbed the stairs, and now in front of them were the machines that handled the many processes necessary in preparing flax for spinning.

He felt a thrill run through him as he realised that this was how his mill could be run, and he resolved to learn as much as possible while he had the chance.

They moved to another area, and watched, fascinated, as bright ribbons of flax reflected the light, iridescent in the semi-darkness, pouring through the machines on the way to the spinners. Women and girls wound the flowing silver into tall cans, and then broke the lines of fibre into three before placing them on the spreading boards.

Somewhere else they saw men take the dried flax and lay it across lengths of wood placed on frames that they beat with a swingler. The flax was then dressed, the fibres being drawn through a series of combs, and the tow removed until the best and longest fibres came out of the final combing.

Then came the spinning looms where women spun the fibre into yarn ready to seam the great sails, their legs pedalling up and down furiously but in perfect rhythm, sitting on stools and working the foot treadles like slaves pulling at oars in a ship's galley, the wheels, belts and flyers keeping the yarn twisting continuously. Tom could smell the sweat as they toiled, and the image of his own mother sitting in the shed with her spinning wheel working steadily to make a few more pennies so that the family could eat, brought tears to his eyes.

He would love to have spent the time of day with these women who were taking such an active part helping the Navy win the war with the French, but conversation was impossible in this noisy place.

But regardless of the denial by Jim Gilbert, he was unprepared for the scene before him. Small children darted under the treacherous machines to retie broken yarn, make minor repairs or to replace bobbins, and he could see traces of blood where they had already been too slow. However, they appeared to be well fed, although it was hard to tell through the thick grey dust that covered their bodies.

Rose too had seen the children, and he moved towards her in a bid to stop her speaking to the foreman, but he failed to see a broom a young girl was pushing around the stone floor and tripped over it.

"I'm sorry," he said as he tried to move out of the way, but the girl ignored him and carried on. It was obvious that she hadn't heard him, and he indicated to Rose that it was time they left. The foreman was approaching, and anxious to avoid him Tom gripped Rose's arm and took her to the top of the stairs.

"What do you think you're doing?" she hissed, as she tried to pull away from him.

"I think it's time we went," he said, forcing her to follow him down the stairs, but when they were nearly at the bottom she twisted away and stood facing him, trembling with fury.

"Why, Tom? Why did you want me to leave?" she screamed at him. "Didn't you see that state of those children?"

"Be quiet," hissed Tom. "Every time you open your mouth you cause me trouble. I don't know what's the matter with you lately. You're ruining everything."

"How dare you! I wish I'd never come to this horrible place."

Rose ran down the last few steps, slammed the factory door behind her and ran out into the lane, and then as if she had second thoughts she stopped running, and waited for him to join her.

Tom followed slowly. Let her wait, he thought. Let her get it out of her system. The last few days had been terrible and the week wasn't over yet. He should never have allowed the situation get so out of hand.

"Jim Gilbert lied, I know," he said simply, when he caught up with her. "Obviously he doesn't think he treats the children badly, but they make him money, and no matter what he says, money to a business man is more important than happy children. There's nothing we can do about it. We need his help, so we shall have to forget about it."

"Tom Welland! I'm ashamed of you," Rose said angrily. "Who's speaking like a hard faced employer now? Would you treat your child labourers like that? Because if you would, I can tell you that I want nothing more to do with you."

"I wouldn't have child labourers in the first place. You know that! But if I interfere now we'll lose all we've worked for. Don't you see?"

She stared at him, and then she shook her head. "No, Tom. I'm sorry, but I don't see, and I never will."

"Can you save your opinions until I tell you my proposition, and perhaps then you will understand why I feel as I do?"

She nodded. "You can try, but I doubt that I shall change my mind."

"Please don't accuse me of being unsympathetic, Rose, but I think you're seeing this problem from a maternal point of view. You're a passionate woman, and seeing the children in this dreadful predicament must have broken your heart. It's hard to choose between business and compassion, but the children are used to harsh conditions, and they'll be so much happier when everyone is working together for the same cause. I'll bet if you opened the door to freedom they wouldn't know what to do."

"Children need to play, to have fun, and to make friends…"

"As so they will, one day. They won't be working in my mill, I promise. You'll see that happier people are healthier people, who will work harder when they see that conditions are improving. In turn business will expand, and their pay will improve. Children won't need to work. Tell you what," he added. "Let's go and find the canal and the hatches that intersect the river, and then we'll go on to Freshwater and the retting ponds."

They stood watching the man who controlled the flow of water to the mill that allowed the meadows to be flooded for early grass production, and then crossed the field bridge above the tranquil pool below the hatches. They were startled as a heron suddenly flew up in front of them, lifting itself on lazy grey wings from the river bank as it rose gracefully into the sky above a group of willow trees and disappeared into the fading light.

It was getting on for four in the afternoon when they finally left the coast road and turned down the narrow stony path towards Freshwater, where retting ponds nestled alongside the river under the cliffs at Golden Cap. For a while they watched the labourers at work, following each process with practised eyes, envying them the freedom of the beach, until the flash of a fish hook claimed Tom's attention. He looked up to witness the fishermen bringing in the mackerel catch, hundreds of silver fish leaping through the water before being flung onto the floor of the boat.

Nearer the shore, men in seine boats were working hard to bring netfuls of fish to the surface. Someone called 'mackerel straying,' and the fishermen pulled strongly on their oars to bring another shoal of fish aboard before the terns, their wings dipping gracefully into the sea took part of the catch. Further along the beach at Bexington tiny black figures hauled in their seine nets, silhouetted against the orange red of the sun as it slowly sank over Golden Cap and Thorncombe Beacon.

They made up on the high cliffs overlooking the sea, and held hands watching the little boats playing tug-of-war with the tide below, as lobster and crab pots bobbed about on the surface. A few tarred lerrets had been left on the beach, but most of the boats had come ashore. A gang of fish tutes passed them as they made their way down the cliff path, empty baskets slung over the backs of their ponies as they made their way towards the women on the beach. The wives gathered at the shoreline waited to load the fish from the boats into deep panniers, their long skirts and aprons sweeping the shingle, their shoulders draped with shawls, their heads obscured by pretty cotton frilled and tucked bonnets. Tom thought what a charming painting the scene would make if it were transferred onto canvas.

The fishing party were singing lustily, for judging by the overfilled baskets they had done an excellent evening's work. As the men and women passed by he could see they were covered in blood and slime and dripping with fish scales. They seemed sublimely happy as they made their way towards the Dove Inn where their ponies grazed on the turf outside. Minutes later the sound of drunken singing reached them, and Tom smiled. These were some of the people who had taken unauthorised leave from the mill in order to make extra money during the fishing season; and in a way he could understand Jim Gilbert's frustration. He would lose a lot of money that summer.

"It'll soon be too dark to look at the warehouses." Tom stood up, ready to go. He surveyed the empty horizon, sighed, and, arm-in-arm, he and Rose made their way back to Emma, who had been grazing on a patch of rough grass.

"I need to see if any of the warehouses are empty, and then I can ask Jim Gilbert who owns them," he said, as he urged Emma on down the rough track.

"I'm not sure how much room I shall need, but that depends on how many businesses want to export their goods," he continued. "If there is not enough room on the ships they can go by chaise mail coach from the Greyhound Hotel in East Street at Bridport. We may be able to import goods from other countries, and machinery can be imported..." Tom broke off, his mind too busy with ideas to voice his thoughts. Rose rarely spoke, wisely allowing him time to make important decisions.

Fog was drifting across the harbour in waves, and the deep resonant tones of the ships' sirens echoed eerily across the water. Bells clanged intermittently, foghorns wailed, and the gentle suck and splash of the water washed the walls of the harbour. All around them the usual mustiness of ropes and rigging and damp sails mixed with the staleness of kegs, casks and barrels, the reek of horse dung and turpentine, but worst of all the all pervasive stink of rotting fish made them both want to retch.

Night was now upon them. Further out at sea ships were silhouetted in the moonlight; muffled shouts and creaking timbers became evident from ships close by, foreign voices drifted down to them from the decks and galleys, and for Tom this was to prove to be the start of a whole new way of life.

The large grey buildings that rose up in front of them made an impressive sight, and Tom ran ahead, running up and down steps, blindly searching for an unlocked door that would lead him to the storerooms. All he needed was just one empty building.

Rose waited in the shadows, listening nervously as she heard footsteps resonate from iron ladders somewhere in the distance, the ever pervasive fog swirling impenetrably about her until she realised that she was losing her sense of direction, and she began to experience real fear.

Suddenly the footsteps drew nearer, and as they came closer her heart beat fiercely in her chest and she started shaking.

"Who…who is it?" she whispered.

"Me of course. Who else?" Tom said as he emerged from the fog, and now she could see that he was grinning.

"Tom. It's not funny," she said angrily. "I was scared, I thought… "

He held her closely and kissed her firmly on the lips to silence her. "No one else is here except us, which is a good thing because I've found enough space to keep us going for a while. As long as no one else puts in a claim it will be ours, as long as we can afford the rent. Then we can start looking for a boat!

"Let's go home," she said.

Rose held tightly to her cloak as blustery winds swept them along the coast road towards Burton, and Emma began to slow as the road became steeper, the trees sparser as freshly sown fields of flax and hemp took their place. Close by were the limestone cliffs, high and dangerous, the seagulls mewing as they floated in the night sky above them, and she was grateful when they moved inland.

Now the hedges were becoming thicker; tall trees were outlined against the skyline, and in the distance Tom could just make out the tall chimney of the spinning mill that rose higher than the church tower, the building seeming to dominate the huddled thatch roofs cowering beneath it, a symbol of the march of industrialisation that would soon sweep all before it. Tom gritted his teeth and determined that the outworkers and families akin to his own who toiled in their own back yards would not lose their livelihoods, trusting that his attempt to convince the mill owner to help them would be successful.

When Tom approached Jim Gilbert about renting warehouse space the mill owner deliberated over his reply, and Tom was becoming increasingly anxious. He was disappointed; the man had promised to help, and now it seemed as if he were backing down. Everything had been

110

going well but now, without space to store the goods, he might as well forget it. Would the same thing happen over the boat, he wondered?

"It seems that I have already promised the use of that particular warehouse to a business colleague," Jim Gilbert said. "I'm afraid that I had forgotten about it, but a promise is a promise, so I must let it go. However, I think there may be another space available within the next couple of weeks and," he said smiling, "it is nearer to the harbour. I am hoping that if I offer my business colleague a fair price I may be able to do a deal with him and to loan one of his boats. Would that be acceptable?"

An idea had been brewing in Rose's mind ever since they had left the mill; there must be something she could do to help the children, surely, even one day of happiness would make a world of difference. She had heard that the King often visited Weymouth to bathe in the sea, so why not take them there?

It was now May, and in a few weeks it would be summer. They would need wagons and carts, food, and permission from the parents who, of course, would be welcome to come. Who could deny these poor little children a treat? She could imagine their excitement; a day away from a life of dirt and hunger, real sand, not the hard pebbles that surrounded the Bay, sea they could paddle in, and most importantly of all, freedom. And to top it all, they would see the King of England. What a privilege, what an experience; they would talk about it with their friends and later with their grandchildren; reliving the excitement of the day they went to Weymouth to see the King. Surely Tom would agree; but would Jim Gilbert?

Chapter 10

A cold, fresh breeze was blowing in from the sea as they made their way into Bridport the following morning.

Rose looked about her with interest as Emma trotted briskly through the broad streets, but she was disappointed to see that the doors of the little terraced houses remained closed, the women evidently preferring to stay beside their fires to braid their nets.

High above the limestone cliffs herring gulls swooped and dived, squawking raucously as they fought over scraps of fishy refuse; not far away great flocks of starlings wheeled about the sky, gradually dropping down into the reed beds at Burton Mere.

"Why is the main street so wide, Tom? You could fit at least two streets of Yeovil into this one."

"D'you see those hooks on the walls of the houses?"

"Yes."

"Ropers hook their twine onto them and in the long narrow alleys stretching back from the main street form the walks," he said, before turning his attention to weaving his way through the traffic.

"Did you know, for instance, that monkeys used to twist vines and make them into primitive hammocks?" he said when they were free of the vehicles blocking the road. "Egyptian fishermen used them long before Christ was born, and it's possible that the earliest sails were made from palm fronds, used in Egyptian boats for shade or decoration. The Romans and the Vikings used hide. Sailcloth was brought here at the end of the sixteenth century, and in sixteen sixty four the King of France wouldn't let anyone in his country export it, which in turn made the English want to manufacture it, mainly in Somerset. Later on it was made in Bristol and Dorchester. Then in seventeen forty-six no British built ship was allowed out of port unless her first suit of sails were purely British. So you see, Rose, we are merely carrying on a tradition for making ships' sails, ropes and nets, and we can tell that because of the account books that have been left behind by these people as the craft has been passed down from father to son. And now, because of all the wars raging on the Continent, and because New Zealand needs ropes and lines for their cod trade, the rope industry is doing very well."

Rose laughed. "The way you tell it, it sounds like you are training to teach in one of those new Dames schools. You could make it sound more interesting."

"I tell it as it is, my love, that's all. It's merely a slice of history that I learned from my father. Hold on a minute." He broke off as a child ran into the road and he hauled on the reins as he swerved to miss him.

"Why don't parents keep their children under control," he growled.

Rose brushed his cheek with her finger. "Thanks to your father you're a very interesting man, d'you know that?" she said softly.

In spite of his irritation, Tom smiled. "You're good for me, you know that, don't you?"

East Street was crowded with country folk who had come into town on business, and although it was not market day business appeared to be brisk, with gigs, curricles and carets littered about the street. Stagecoaches queued outside the Greyhound Hotel waiting for businessmen to conclude their meetings.

Rose breathed deeply, taking in the fresh sea air.

"I can smell the sea from here, Tom, and it makes my nose tingle. There's a strong smell of fish, too, and it's mixed with the tang of smoke. And what's that low rumbling noise in the distance?"

"It's the sound of the waves dragging back from the shingle below the cliffs," Tom explained. "Sometimes the breakers crash over the pebbles, the water bubbles and boils; spray is thrown up and is then drawn back, so it's not surprising that there are so many shipwrecks."

Rose frowned. "Have many men been killed?"

"Quite a few. The Chesil coast can be frightening and dangerous, especially for the men who have been pressed into service and forced to serve on ships without any idea how to sail them." Tom sighed. "It's a hard life."

"I want to take those children to Weymouth," she said bluntly. "They need some fun in their boring lives.

Tom turned to look at her, his eyebrows raised in surprise.

"Do you think that's wise? Jim Gilbert won't like it at all, and we don't want to upset him just now. We need him on our side, Rose, not against us."

"Is there a way we can persuade him, perhaps?"

"There is no way he would allow his mill to grind to a halt so that a few children can 'play' for the day."

"How about asking those fishing tutes if they would promise not to leave their work at the mill for at least a month, if we in turn could offer them all a day at the seaside with their children? Surely Jim Gilbert would agree to that? He wouldn't lose money, or production. In fact, he would gain by it."

"I doubt Jim Gilbert would believe his workers if they presented him with such a proposition. And I'm not sure that his workers would want to lose their extra money."

"Hm. That could be a problem," admitted Rose. "Perhaps they could offer to fish for two weeks instead of four."

"That would allow them to make some money, I suppose."

"We'll have to ask them, but as I have said before, Tom, happy workers are better workers. Everyone's happier after a little holiday. Jim Gilbert and his wife could come if they wanted."

"I think that's going a bit far, Rose, but I can see that you feel strongly about this."

"Passionately," she agreed.

"And if I don't suggest it, you will?"

"Absolutely."

Jim Gilbert refused to listen to Rosie's plea. "I'm not surprised that it was you who suggested it," he said angrily. "Do you realise that you are in grave danger of losing my help? I hope you haven't mentioned this idea to the children of Burton, because once they hear about it we will have a riot on our hands. I wish you would get those children out of your mind. Take your own. I'm sure they will enjoy it."

"I'm sorry if I upset you," Rose said. "I seem to have a habit of doing that, but I can assure you that I did consider your interests as well."

"How?"

"Well, if you let them have a day off, perhaps they will promise to take only two weeks for fishing, instead of four."

Jim sighed. "Why is it that women can't control their maternal instincts? Tom, Can't you help her?"

"You're not listening to me," said Rose angrily. "I think it's a good idea."

"Highly impractical," said Jim Gilbert. "Who would look after the children, and how would everybody manage if they lost a day's pay?"

"The parents would look after their own children, and they could make up the time later."

"When?"

Rose smiled. "My point exactly, Mr Gilbert. "You are admitting that your labourers work so many hours that they do not have time to make up for one lost day."

"Not at all, Mrs Howard. "They have plenty of time off. Anyway," he blustered, "I think you should mind your own business. The answer is no, no, no. All right?"

"All right." Rose smiled again. And then she walked away, leaving Tom and the mill owner to discuss the subject, as she knew they would.

"Blooming cheek," muttered Jim Gilbert.

"I do apologise," said Tom, realising that Rose had managed to convince him to do as she wanted in the only way a woman can; deviously.

"All we need now is to find out the date the King is due to go to Weymouth," Rose said with a smile.

"You're a crafty woman," Tom said affectionately. "You always get your own way."

"You can tell the children if you like. Bring smiles to their faces. Give them something to look forward to."

Half a dozen tipcarts were loaned by farmers. They had grumbled at first, for how were they to manage their harvest without the means to carry the hay?

"It's only for the day," Rose had said persuasively. "Think of the children's happy faces."

One by one they had relented, saying they would manage somehow. Aaron Smith provided the horses to pull the wagons, their food and water, and soon the whole village was putting the finishing touches to the arrangements.

The children from Burton Bradstock yelled in excitement as two wagons rolled to a stop in the High Street. Parents stood with their children, awaiting their turn to climb up and sit on the hay bales inside.

"We ain't going to no seaside," shouted little Jimmy Baines. "I bet they're taking us back to the hayfield to work instead, and that ain't fair."

"Sit down or you'll fall out," Tom said sternly. He tugged at the reins, and they were off. But they didn't get far.

"We don't know you," shouted five-year-old George Dixon. "Where've you come from?"

"Yeah. You ain't me father. You can't tell me what to do." A boy with a head of thick curls threw a stone at Tom, hitting him on the back of the head.

Tom stopped the cart in the middle of the road and climbed down.

"Who did that?" he demanded.

No one owned up.

"I don't know why I bother," he growled.

"I don't want to go," howled a two-year-old girl. "Daddy. That man's nasty. I want to go home."

Several of the children started to climb over the sides of the wagon, and Tom swore in frustration. "For God's sake, Rose. Can't you make the parents control their children? "

"I'm doing the best I can," she mumbled, as she helped them retrieve their offspring from the roadside.

"It's not an empty threat," Tom warned. "A lot of people have worked hard to give everyone this treat. I might as well know now, are we going or not?"

Rose was trying to balance on a hay bale between two little boys, and she felt far from comfortable, but this had been her idea, and she was desperate to see it through.

"Don't you want to see the King?" she asked the children.

George stuck out his bottom lip. "Don't care. Don't want to see no King. That ain't no treat. I don't trust no-one."

Rose glared at him. "You ungrateful child. I wish we'd saved our money."

"It isn't that the children aren't grateful," one of the mothers explained gently. "Working in the mill is all they know. They're scared of change, but I'm sure by the end of the day they'll realise how lucky they've been and find how much they've enjoyed themselves."

"Well. I want to go to the seaside and play in the sand," said John Lucas," a lad from Gilbert's mill. "Fishing ain't as exciting as this."

"We're going to build sand castles and have a picnic on the beach, and we want you to have fun." Rose smiled. "But if you are lucky enough to see the King I want you all to be good. He won't take kindly to a bunch of rude children. Sit quietly, or else you'll frighten the animals. Now, do we go home, or go on to Weymouth."

"Weymouth," roared the children.

The horses tossed their heads and rattled their harnesses; the brightly coloured ribbons on their manes were blowing in the breeze, and the clip clop of their hooves sounded hollow as they trotted over uneven cobbles on their way to the open country.

When they left the confines of the village, the children ignored Tom and clambered over each other in excitement, eager to see over the hedges to the fields beyond, where sheep and cows grazed under the trees.

As they approached Weymouth clouds of dust rose into the air as fully laden carriages passed them on their way to the resort, sometimes with barely a hair's breadth between them. They passed soldiers marching towards the coast, regiment by regiment, the colours of their uniforms adding formality to the occasion.

"One of the fishermen told me that Prince Frederick, the Duke of York may be here today," explained one of the fathers. "There's going to be a big parade, and his younger brothers, the Dukes of Kent, Cambridge and Sussex will be going, too. The number of troops has been increased because of the threat from France, and because the King is worried about his family's safety."

"Look, over there, above the sea wall," said Rose suddenly, pointing towards several ships anchored in the bay on her left. "Does anyone know what they are?"

"That's the Royal Sovereign, the King's yacht," replied Fred Parsons, one of the hecklers. "And amongst the frigates surrounding it are the Augusta and the Charlotte, the Aeolus and the Crescent."

After the wagons, carts and drays came citizens on foot; patriotic but footsore men, women and children wearing caps decorated with the motto "God Save the King." The Burton children raised their own homemade flags and banners and shouted and waved as they entered the town, with Rose and the other mothers trying to maintain order as they jumped up and down trying to see if the royal family had arrived.

Many people had assembled in front of the greenery-bedecked houses; bouquets and garlands were being thrown into the road to herald the royal carriage entering Weymouth from the opposite direction.

The wagons were abandoned at the nearest available inn, and Tom collected his party together to issue instructions.

"Each child must stay with its parents, so no-one should get lost in the crowd. We will meet on the steps by the esplanade in about half an hour and wait there until everyone is accounted for. Until then, have fun."

The group dispersed and Tom, Rose, Emily and Ben made their way to the front of the throng of people, hoping to find the best position to see the King.

"There they are," Tom shouted, as the royal carriage appeared around a bend in the road. As it entered the Turnpike, the key bugle announced the arrival of the royal family, but it was immediately drowned by the cheering crowds and the town band playing 'God Save the King.'

There was a wild surge as countless admirers attempted to move closer to the royal party as they approached Gloucester Lodge, but they were held back by soldiers as the King was helped down the steps. He shook the hand of the beaming mayor who, dressed in his official robes, was bowing deeply.

"I wonder what they're saying," whispered Rose.

"A well prepared speech, I should imagine," replied Tom.

"I'll bet he's asking him why he's wearing a green eyeshade," Ben said, too loudly.

"Shhhh..." warned his father. "I expect he's got bad eyesight, but he doesn't need you to point it out."

"I've heard he's going blind."

"Going mad, more like."

Ben seized on the speculation, determined to fuel the fire.

"Is the King mad, dad?" His eyes shone in anticipation of the prospect of the monarch leaping about, screaming, and falling down the steps.

"I don't think so, son. He's getting old, like the rest of us."

Suddenly shots from shore batteries at Portland Castle rang out, drowning Tom's words. Simultaneously flags were hoisted all over the town.

Everyone gasped at the splendour of it all, and for many, tears of patriotism were shed. The rapturous welcome for the King proved that he was still as popular as ever, despite rumours circulating that that he was, indeed, mad, a fact that Tom considered high unlikely, as it was well known that he had lost control over his sons and was becoming increasing frail. As far as Tom was concerned he was loved for his piety, his dignity and his honesty.

What did concern him was the build up of troops and local volunteer forces mingling with the people along the length of the esplanade. Their uniforms added colour and excitement, but to Tom it meant that war was looming. The amount of ships and frigates anchored in the bay added credence to his theory, and he was aware that the presence of the King's second son, the Duke of York, accompanied by his younger brothers would heighten the need for strict security.

Notices warning that drays and carriages were restricted in the town were being torn to shreds by vehicles being driven through the tightly packed streets, and Tom's blood ran cold. In such a crowd an incident involving the use of firearms could prove highly dangerous, especially for the families of Burton that he had unwittingly encouraged to enjoy a day out at the seaside

But they were here now, and he would have to be extra vigilant; as soon as he suspected a threat he would round them up and take them home as quickly as possible.

Chapter 11

The King had returned to his rooms at Gloucester Lodge, and the children scampered down the steps to the beach.

The tide was out, and the coastline stretched for miles. The children kicked off their shoes and ran, whooping and laughing through the fine golden sand, their eyes wide with excitement. The parents watched from a distance, thrilled that their offspring had been given this chance for a holiday, all too brief, but welcome just the same.

The children brought out an assortment of buckets and wooden spoons and soon sandcastles were sprouting up all over the beach.

"Mum." Emily's voice was insistent. "Charlie's gone. He said he wanted to fetch some water to make a moat around his castle, and he hasn't come back."

"Where's his mother?"

"She's gone to look for him."

"Charlie can't swim," Rose cried, visibly distressed. "I'd better tell Tom; he'll go and look for him."

Tom was momentarily unaware of an eerie echo from the past that seemed to relentlessly pursue him as he sped towards the shoreline, closely followed by Rose. He shaded his eyes with his hand and scanned the vast body of water, but so many bathers were enjoying themselves it was impossible to tell if Charlie was amongst them.

When Tom's feet hit the water, he was surprised to find that it only came up to his ankles. Evidently the sea at Weymouth, unlike the uncertain depth of the sea at Burton, was shallow for as far as the eye could see. But Charlie could not swim, and it was possible that he could have drowned, unseen amongst all the trampling feet.

As he searched, more and more bathers kicked off their shoes, discarding clothing as modesty allowed and paddled into the shallows, splashing each other, screaming in new found delight as the cold droplets touched their sun warmed skin. The Burton party stood in small groups, talking animatedly.

The boy's mother, having questioned the other parents about her son's disappearance, pulled off her footwear and ran into the sea to join Tom, her only hope. Her face was streaked with tears, and he wished that he had better news for her.

But now the sound of cheering made them look up. The King had emerged from the Lodge and was coming down the steps, his guards close by in case of trouble. He headed for his bathing machine, the gaily-decorated boat that was being towed into the water by a couple of horses, so that he could enter the sea in privacy.

The machine was certainly a sight to behold! Oblong at the base, painted white with blue and red panels and cornices, the semi-circle at the top decorated with a crown. At the back of the contraption the British flag was flying at the top of a pole at least ten feet high, with a painting of the King's Arms occupying the place in front of it.

The Queen's bathing machine, a more sombre affair, had already been drawn into the sea. It was close enough for Tom and Rose to see the ladies of the royal family sitting inside looking through telescopes, focussing upon the public who were watching them from the shoreline.

The beach was coming alive, and all eyes followed the royal family, who were leaving their bathing machines and plunging bravely into the sea, their dresses tucked into their flannel underwear.

All this had drawn the attention away from the search; Tom and the child's mother, Violet Blake, were becoming more and more distraught as swimmers enjoyed themselves in the water, unaware that a tragedy was about to unfold around them.

Tom took charge of the situation. "Ahoy there!" he called, waving his arms and shouting to attract their attention, but his efforts fell on deaf ears.

"Please help us," shouted Mrs Blake, again and again until she was hoarse, and eventually someone pointed to one of the bathing machines barely feet away from them.

Tom paddled towards it, and now he could see that Charlie was about to climb inside, and he waded towards him.

"Out you get, young man," he said, twisting Charlie Blake's ear until he obeyed.

"Oh, I do apologise," Tom said, as the door opened to reveal one of the queen's ladies in waiting in the middle of her toilette. "He's a little inquisitive, I'm afraid," he said, and dragged the boy away and closed the door.

"Don't you realise how worried we were, Charlie?" he said angrily. Your poor mother thought you'd drowned, you stupid boy."

"I wanted to see what kind of underwear the lady had on." The boy grinned cheekily, and despite his frustration, Tom repressed the urge to smile.

"You shouldn't have gone near the sea, let alone the machines," Tom said angrily. "You've ruined the day for your mother, and your father won't be too pleased with you either. Go back with her to the beach, and don't you dare run away again, or you'll be in real trouble."

Rose joined him, and frowned when Tom told her what had happened. "That young lad's a bit of a rascal," she said. "The other children are too frightened to go near the water."

The sea was now full of people anxious to be near their sovereign, wearing hats with the motif 'God Save the King' on their bonnets and their girdles, while even further out large hooded umbrellas bobbed about, concealing those bathers who preferred to swim in complete privacy.

Suddenly a band hidden inside one of the machines struck up the royal anthem, playing the tune relentlessly whenever the King raised his head above the water.

"That's the funniest thing I've seen for a long time," Rose said, laughing. "That's taking loyalty too far!"

"There are a lot of troops about today, Tom said casually. "Can you see that unit over there, at the Portland end of the beach? They look as if they're patrolling the sands. I overheard someone on the esplanade saying that King George's own Hanoverian troops are here; I believe one regiment is at Dorchester, and the German Light Dragoons are at Radipole Barracks."

"There seem to be a lot of royal Naval vessels on duty in the bay, too," Rose said thoughtfully. "It has to be more than coincidence, surely. What d'you think is going on, Tom?"

"I'm not sure," he said. "I'll go for a stroll and see if someone can give me some answers."

"And I'll go and have a word with the parents," Rose said.

It was picnic time, and the women were sharing out the food, the men handing out mugs of milk.

She walked towards them. "Can you gather around me a moment please?"

"But the food…"

"That's all right, Sam, it won't take long," she said determinedly. "Tom suspects that the presence of so many troops could mean trouble. He's gone to find out, and I need to know if you want to stay here or would you rather go home. How many of you want to stay?"

Ten people raised their hands.

"How many want to go home?"

Six pairs of hands were raised.

"So we stay. But if we do, I would like the children kept to a small area of the beach, and watched continually, as we don't want a repeat of children wandering into the sea. I couldn't bear it if anyone drowned. Are you prepared to do that?"

They all nodded.

"And if there is a problem we must leave immediately. All right?"

It was decided that a sandcastle competition would be held, and whilst the children were busy Rose and Dorothy, one of the mothers she had befriended, decided to make their way to the town, where they could browse in the shop windows and observe the wealthy visitors who were taking advantage of the luxury goods and souvenirs. It would also be a good vantage point for Rose to look out over the bay and watch the ships floating at anchor and keep a look out for signs of trouble. But first she needed to speak to Ben and Emily.

"Now, Ben. You are old enough to understand what you have been told, aren't you?"

Ben nodded. "I shan't let Emily, or any of the other children go near the sea," he said seriously.

"You're sure?"

Ben nodded.

"If I go to the town you'll stay on the beach and build sandcastles?"

"I promise Mummy."

Rose wandered amongst the crowds, watching as prizes of silk and lace were swept up and carried back to hotels by people taking advantage of the sedan chairs, carried high to prevent the well-dressed shoppers muddying their clothing.

Dorothy suddenly dived into a bookshop and started rummaging amongst the shelves. Excitedly she pulled out a small booklet entitled 'King George and His Family at Weymouth.'

Rose peered over her shoulder as Dorothy turned the pages, but the writing was small and barely legible. "Come over to the window," she suggested. "We'll be able to see it better there. Look, there's a bench underneath it where we can sit."

But she had another motive for the move. The window was so positioned that she would be able to look out on the troops walking through the crowd. When she could prise Dorothy away from the book perhaps they should think of going back, and then if an alarm were raised they would be near to the beach to collect the children and lead them to safety.

Tom was watching and waiting from another vantage point, ready to act in response to a threat, and would head for the Burton party on the sands immediately it happened. He had not wanted to alarm Rose until he was certain there was a problem. To him, family security was his most important objective; the King, the prime target, would be well protected by others. The parents would take care of their own, but as soon as he was convinced trouble was apparent, he would warn the rest of the party instantly.

Dorothy opened the book at the front page.

"It seems that Gloucester Lodge has been the royal family's favourite residence since seventeen-eighty-nine," she read, "and it was from there that they would visit either the ballroom or the theatre, or indulge in sea bathing. King George the third has entertained Prime Ministers Pitt and Addington in the audience chamber of the hotel, the British Commander of Corsica and other celebrities, but lately his madness is beginning to set him apart from his interest in affairs of state. The King is devoted to his fifteen children, especially the girls, whom he regards with passionate affection and calls them his 'Cordelias.' His relationship with his boys is different, and he is unable to come to terms with the licentious behaviour of his eldest son. Owing to his failing health he is retiring more and more from politics, but he is resolute in his determination to maintain the struggle with France."

"Where did you learn to read like that?" Rose said admiringly. "Tom's been teaching me, and I'm doing fine. I'm better at doing the accounts, though. He wouldn't do anything unless he asked me first."

Oh dear. She hadn't meant to lie, but she felt no shame. Dorothy was an intelligent and confident person. She needed her to think well of her, there was nothing wrong in that; it was important for her to be thought an able partner to Tom.

Dorothy, however, was indifferent to Rose's vanity, anxious to promote her own interests.

"My Albert taught me," she said proudly, "but he joined the local infantry a year ago, so it's important for me to manage things when he's away." She sighed, but continued reading aloud. Suddenly she looked up, her brow furrowed with anxiety.

"It seems then, that although the King feels he is too old for politics, he is in favour of war with France. He thinks that entrepreneurs will force their way ahead and move away from regal control, and form their kind of world based on industrial power, and it won't be long before George the Fourth claims the throne. What a terrible thought, Dorothy. The man who will become Prince Regent is a very wasteful and greedy man, and I certainly don't want him as our next King. But I think the person who wrote this is right about industrial power. It's going to happen, whether we like it or not, and we must do our best to keep up with it."

"What's your Tom want to do, besides making his sails?" asked Dorothy. "I know it's an awful thing to talk about, but I think the men feel they have to do their share towards the protection of their country."

"I agree with you. Tom's determined to go to sea, and he'd be proud to sail with Nelson, the sailor he admires the most."

"My brother Robert is helping to man one of the signal stations, intercepting signals received from passing ships."

Dorothy moved her head slightly and now Rosie found that she had a better view of the beach. She could see that all the children were playing happily in the sand and had no need of her for the moment.

"It appears that for a long time Nelson's fleet has been trying to entice foreign fleets out of Toulon, but his ships are becoming unseaworthy and the men are tired. All Nelson can do is to provide his men with fresh fruit and vegetables and keep up their morale."

"So it's just a matter of waiting then."

"It would seem that way, Dorothy agreed. "But he says that Pierre Villeneuve, the Captain of the French fleet, should be worried. Britain's ships are faster and full of the best-trained men in the world, able to fire twice as fast as the enemy. After winning the Battle of the Nile Nelson can do no wrong, and now he's regarded as a hero; brave, daring, quick thinking, and brilliant at fooling the enemy. Robert's convinced that we'll win any battle with Nelson in charge of it." Suddenly she gasped and her body tensed.

"What was that?"

"A flash. I saw a flash," she said breathlessly. "Are they shooting at each other d'you think?"

Rose followed her gaze to where a brig was riding at anchor out at sea, and although it was difficult to see through the intermittent fog, which seemed to have suddenly descended, there appeared to be feverish activity on deck.

"Possibly. And I think it's flying a French flag, although I can't make out its name. What the hell is going on?"

Then in the distance came the beating of a drum, the pounding of hoof beats coming nearer and nearer until the cavalry was swarming all over the esplanade, with some of the riders dismounting and running into the sea to escort the royal family to safety.

"The children," gasped Rose. "I hope we're not too late."

As Rose and Dorothy left the shop and hurried along the esplanade, they could see that horses were being put to the royal carriages outside Gloucester Lodge ready to whisk the King and his family away. They were caught up in a mass of scudding feet and hooves as people pushed their way towards the steps that would take them away from the beach, but before they could reach them a horse came galloping out of control along the seashore, splashing through the bathers, and the women watched in horror as the children and their parents fled for their lives, running in all directions along the beach, trampling their sandcastles into the sand.

King George and his family were covered in blankets, bundled into the waiting royal carriages outside the Lodge and taken away, whilst on the beach the children screamed in terror.

The cavalry were in disarray, but then a man leapt onto a riderless horse and pursued the runaway until he managed to drive it into the sea, slowing it down until he was able to grab the reins.

Rose watched in amazement, her hand over her mouth. "That was Tom, I'm sure of it," she exclaimed. "He risked his life for those bathers. He's mad, absolutely mad!"

"Is he all right?" gasped Dorothy. "He's fallen and he's not getting up."

Rose started to move towards him, but her friend held her back.

"Don't get in the way," she warned. "Tom won't thank you for it."

"Yes he is, look," Rose cried, and started running towards him. But as she reached him she froze, a look of horror on her face. Tom was lying face down in the sand, but when she bent down and rolled him over she could see that there was a deep wound that stretched across his left cheek. She reached out to touch it. "What have you done to yourself?" she asked tenderly.

He pushed her hand away. "Don't," he said abruptly.

"You could have been killed."

"I'm fine," he said brusquely. "But I'm more worried about the children. Where's Ben and Emily? I thought they were with you."

Rose paled, and grabbed his arm. "I thought you had them," she said, suddenly feeling faint. "We have to find them. They'll be so frightened."

Tom was in pain, but he said nothing. He would live. The pain in his side would go, and the wound on his cheek would heal. He had been winded, that was all. With Rose's help, he managed to stand, and he shaded his eyes with his hand as he scanned the beach. It was empty.

"That bathing machine over there. I thought I saw a flash of blue. I wonder if anyone's inside," he said.

"Emily was wearing a blue top," Rose said excitedly. "Ben might be in there too."

His feet sank into the soft, powdery sand as he ran, leaving no footprints. Rose saw him open the door of the machine, reach inside, and come away carrying a child she didn't recognise."

"That's Billy," shrieked Dorothy. "He's found my boy! Billy! Mummy's coming!" she called "Wait for me, my darling. "

132

Rose watched her go, pleased that her friend had found her son, but at the same time, bewildered. Slowly she turned away, and then she crumpled, her face wet with tears. "But where are our children?" she screamed. "Where have they gone?" And she sank to her knees, sobbing hysterically.

"They've drowned, haven't they?" she moaned, swaying back and forth, her eyes closed, as she tried to come to terms with her apparent loss. She felt the warmth from Tom's body as he sat down beside her, and she turned to him blindly, holding out her arms, hoping it had all been a dream, and that he would put her daughter into them, as he had done once before, and then she would hear Ben's merry laugh. But this was not a dream. Their children were dead. There was no other explanation.

"I don't know where they are, Rose, love. Really I don't," he said helplessly. "This day out is turning into a terrible nightmare!"

"Emily won't make it a second time." Tears slid down Rose's cheeks and he stemmed them with his fingers.

"We don't know that, do we, love?" he said gently. "They'll be around here somewhere, you'll see."

But the beach was deserted. The French boats had gone. One or two bathing machines lay upturned, several umbrellas had floated out to sea, their occupants long gone.

Tom stood up and helped Rose to her feet. He was unwilling to go, but there was no reason to stay. Unable to believe their loss, he supported Rose as they walked away, but they hadn't gone far before she stumbled, and as Tom caught her in his arms he looked down, and there in the sand lay Emily's hair ribbon.

Rose bent down and picked it up. She closed her eyes and held it to her cheek, tears springing unbidden to her eyes as she breathed in her daughter's scent. Tom gathered her to him, tears streaming down his face as he remembered the son he had lost. He hated ribbons. For him, they always seemed to be associated with loss.

"We'd better go and find the others," he said miserably, and made his way towards the steps, Rose following numbly.

The streets of Weymouth were silent now; everyone had hidden behind closed doors, leaving the troops to deal with the emergency. The troubled pair returned to the inn they had left so happily several hours before.

Sombre faces greeted their arrival; childless parents huddled together in a corner. No one spoke. There was nothing to say. Their eyes, red and swollen, told their own story.

But Tom was angry. These people had given up; he was no better. He wanted answers, and set about getting them.

"Are we going to sit here while our children are drowning?" he demanded. "Don't you think we should go and look for them? For goodness' sake. The water is so shallow I would have thought that if they had drowned their bodies would have been evident, and I haven't seen any. We may be able to save them, wherever they are, and anyway, the current wouldn't have had time to drag them away just yet. Come on. Get moving. Let's form a search party. We can't just sit here."

"But it isn't safe," protested one of the fathers. "What if there's more shooting? I'll bet them Frenchmen are out there now, waiting for us to show our faces. Sorry, Tom, I'm staying put."

There was a murmur of agreement, and in a fury Tom moved to the centre of the group.

"Listen, you lot. Rose and I have been out there. There is no danger. The French ships have gone, I can assure you. The King has gone. The purpose of the enemy is to kill him, and he's not stupid enough to return, so we shall be quite safe."

Reluctantly the fathers moved towards the door, but before they could step outside, the mayor entered, the missing children not far behind, wet and bedraggled.

"Emily! Ben! Thank God you're safe! Have either of you been hurt?" Rose rushed to the two children and flung her arms around them, and Tom embraced them all. For a while they were oblivious to the other parents being reunited with their children, thankful that their own were safe. And then to stop the children shivering they were presented with blankets provided by the establishment.

The mayor was thanked profusely; and food and drink offered, but as Tom looked around at the sombre faces of the children, he doubted whether they would be able to forget their terrifying experience.

"The King is safe for now," said the Mayor, as he accepted a small beer. "There has been an attempt on his life. I was sitting in the library reading the newspapers, trying to catch up with the week's events, when these children come running past as if the devil was after them. Well," he said, taking a sip of his beer, "realising they have been caught in the stampede on the beach, I took them inside and waited until everything quietened down, and then I asked them where they should be. Fortunately, this little lad here," he said, ruffling Ben's hair, "was bright enough to remember the name of this place, so here we all are."

So now, the mayor, still clad in his ceremonial robes, and surrounded by interested and relieved faces, embarked upon his story.

"Some fishermen got lost in the fog and found themselves in the middle of a large fleet of foreign ships. Immediately they pulled towards land, and once beached, woke a quarryman, who galloped to the ferry, and was shot at along the Chesil Beach. Those Frenchmen must have been dreadful shots because, thank goodness, they missed him. When all was clear he brought the news to Weymouth. The sentinels stationed near the shore say there were many more French ships about, so if I were you, I would take your children out of harms way as soon as you can."

As Tom counted the children onto the wagons, he had no way of knowing that on that very same day Admiral Lord Nelson, cruising off Cadiz with the British fleet was laying before his officers a plan of attack on the Spanish and French fleets.

Chapter 12

For a long time, both the French and British navies had fought for the command of the sea, but where French beliefs tore its Navy apart, the British people had great respect for theirs. Political liberty was synonymous with trade and empire; taxes from goods were paid to finance the Navy and to maintain its fleets to protect Britain from privateers and rival nations. At one time two hundred and fifty warships defended its liberty. Barnacles were scraped from the bottom of ships, their insides lined with strips of copper to improve their speed.

During the French Revolution, Jacobin terror royalist sailors were denounced and killed, and three-quarters of its officers were sent into exile or guillotined. Chaos reigned in its dockyards, ships sailed without routine repairs, there was a shortage of supplies, and ships sank.

By seventeen ninety-four Napoleon was on the French coast with specially built barges, waiting to bring his large army across the Channel to invade Britain.

Admiral Villeneuve had been chosen to lead the French fleet, but he did not share Nelson's love of the sea, or his tactical skills; Napoleon had been victorious in his land battles against the best troops in Europe, and considered Britain a defeated and subservient nation, desperate for peace. Whilst he had been building up his arsenals, Addington, the British Prime Minister, had halved the British army, demobilised the volunteers, paid off more than half of the Navy's hundred battleships, and discharged experienced seamen. Surplus war stores were sold to the highest bidders, often French agents who shipped them across the Channel, where Napoleon was waiting, ready to pounce.

The aim of the taciturn and diminutive Corsican, who spoke no French, was to free the island of Corsica from the domination of France, and to conquer the world. Britain was in the way, and must be defeated.

The silence of the countryside gave Tom a sense of peace. He was on his way home with his girl by his side, their children asleep in the back of the wagon. He looked down at her now, peacefully sleeping, and realised how much he loved her. He had never thought it possible that he could be lucky enough to love again; Rebecca had been all he had ever needed. But now Rose was in his life, and he was more than satisfied.

The turmoil of the past two weeks had exhausted them both; he had accomplished more than he had ever dreamed, and he had found warehouse space so that he could export his goods. The child labourers' outing had turned out unexpectedly, the terrifying end to the day had shocked them all, but thank heavens, none of them had been hurt, and they would have an remarkable tale to tell their grandchildren.

Dawn broke as they broached Beaminster Down, a rosy fingered flush of light filtered through the trees as the sun came up over the hill, prompting the birds' chorus to fill the hills and valleys with song. Rose and the children were asleep, so for a while, it seemed as if this impromptu extravaganza was for his ears only, and lifted his spirits so that he was whistling happily as he descended the hill, knowing he would soon be home, and then he could put into practice everything he had learned. He trusted the men he had left in charge, and soon he would be able to see the result of their efforts.

Half-formed plans began to take shape in his mind as he visualized the future so that he barely noticed the vixen slink home to her young, or the sheep grazing in the fertile pasture. A time for peace after the violent happenings of the day before.

"Farmer Brown's barn has gone!"

Rose had woken, and its loss had taken her by surprise. She surveyed the darkened patch of untidy vegetation, wondering why the farmer had had cause to remove it.

"I wonder if Ned Brown would rent us the land if he doesn't need it," Tom said thoughtfully. "There must be about three acres, I should think. If we borrowed a couple of oxen and a plough to tidy it up, we could sow flax seed on it. Hang on," he said, concentrating on the road as he steered around the final sharp bend, before entering the busy high street, not unusual for mid-day. Old friends raised their hands in greeting, and they waved back, happy to be home.

"Sounds a good idea to me," Rose said, as the wagon slid to a stop in front of their cottage.

"It could solve one of our problems," Tom said, as he released the mare from the wagon and let her into a field.

To his surprise his mother emerged from the doorway, wearing an apron over her muslin dress, her sleeves rolled up to the elbows, and now Tom could see that her hair had been cut short, and what's more, it suited her. She looked younger, somehow.

She walked towards them, smiling, and the stiffness in her joints was less noticeable now; her skin clear of the rash that had afflicted her for as long as he could remember, and the haunted look that had developed after his father's death seemed to have gone.

Tom had not expected his mother to return for some months yet, but it was good to see her. He couldn't wait to tell her his plans for the business, although he realised that it would take time for her to adjust to the new ways of working. But her spirit was strong, and no doubt once she could see the benefits she would throw herself into the new venture with enthusiasm.

Nancy appeared with the children, who greeted their respective parents with a kiss, and then, unconcerned, ran off to play catch with the early fallers under the apple trees.

"How was Bridport?" Mary asked, as the three of them strolled along by the stream.

"Fine, as always."

"Why did you go?"

For goodness sake, thought Tom. She's forgotten already. Father's death must have caused her to lose her memory.

"I needed to see if I could find warehouse space at the docks," Tom said patiently. "I met the owner of a local mill, Jim Gilbert. I learned a lot from the way he ran his mill, and I found a warehouse where we could keep our goods before they're exported. The only thing I didn't find was a boat."

"So you intend to go ahead then."

Tom looked surprised. "Of course. That was the idea."

Mary gripped his arm, and her nails bit into his flesh. "Don't you think it's rather ambitious, son? I know how defensive business men can be, and you might stir up more trouble than you bargained for."

"Mother," Tom said gently, "I know you don't like what I'm doing, but I will make it work, I promise."

Tom walked away, but then he came back. He would try one more time to make her understand, but if she didn't, there was nothing he could do about it.

"We need to work together to pool our resources, and I'm hoping that Samuel Sparks of Viney Bridge over at Crewkerne will see that, and some of the other businesses too. Considering that not so long ago weavers used to trudge all the way to Bristol to sell their cloth, they've come a long way since then. Richard Hayward has a factory at Bridge House at West Chinnock. And don't forget Mr Randall from our own village. We need to establish some kind of trade agreement, so the sooner I get things moving, the better. I wish I'd thought of it before, and then you and father could have had an easier time of it. Everything will be fine, you wait and see. The industrial age you're so worried about will help us, not ruin us. You and father never failed me, so don't mention it again."

"But don't you see, Tom?" Mary flicked a corner of her apron at a swarm of gnats. "We were happy enough as we were. He started the twine works when you were a baby. It was to be something for you to build on in the future. And then you had a child of your own with Rebecca, and you were so happy."

Mary glanced at Rose, expecting a reaction, but there was none, so she continued. "And then she died, and we wondered how you would cope. And we have been proud of you, son, real proud. You have repaid us ten times over. Life hasn't been easy for any of us, and over the next few months I'm sure it will get even harder, when you'll have to leave us and go to fight for our country. But now I want to speak to Rose, so perhaps you'd like to stretch your legs. I should imagine the driving seat in that old wagon isn't too comfortable."

As Tom walked away, Mary sat down on the little stone wall, and looked up at Rose.

"Come and sit next to me, " she invited. "I want to get to know you a little better. I'm pleased that you're still with Tom," she said kindly. "How do you feel about him, my dear?"

Rose was surprised by her frankness, but knowing that she was under scrutiny, the answer she gave would determine her position both in the business and in Tom's life.

"I love him," she said simply. "I've known him for some time now, and I'd like to say I understand him, but there are times when he surprises me, and shows me a side of him that I've never seen before. We've had our arguments, but they've never lasted long, and I'd like to think that he trusts me as much as I trust him."

"How do you feel about a long term commitment?" Mary was watching Rose intently. Would she answer immediately, showing her conviction, or would she hesitate?

"I want to help him make a success of his business," Rose replied at once. "I think his idea is good. If we are to produce the amount of canvas available to the Navy we have to set to work immediately. Competition can be a good thing, and we all have to work together for the same cause."

'Tom and I.' Mary liked the sound of that. The two of them worked well together, and that was good, but Rose's lack of jealousy towards Rebecca puzzled her. Perhaps her commitment was to the business and not to her son. However, her daughter Emily was a delightful child and made a good companion for Ben. Reluctantly she was forced to admit that Rose would fit in.

"The table is set for lunch, my dear," she said now. "And afterwards I want to show you the changes I've made to the kitchen."

Mary rose from her seat on the wall and scuttled back to the cottage, belying the fact that she was almost fifty, and supposedly crippled with pain.

Rose smiled. It seemed as if she had been accepted into the Welland family, but something was bothering her. She followed more slowly, unable to rid herself of a feeling of apprehension. What would Mary say when she found out that she had no idea how to do the accounts?

The kitchen had been transformed. Once untidy and shabby, it was now comfortable and homely, with new curtains at spotless windows, darned matting on the stone floor and pictures the children had drawn covering the walls. Cane chairs surrounded a rickety wooden table, and various stools were scattered about the room

But most of all Rose was surprised by the number of shelves adorning the walls, overflowing with coloured yarns Pots of brightly coloured liquid filled the whole of one windowsill, and below it was a long wooden box crammed with dried flowers, wood, bark, nuts and leaves.

"What d'you think?" Mary asked, anxious for her approval. "I've been trying out different kinds of weaving, see, to brighten everything up, and now I've started selling things to people in the village. I look for bits and pieces when I go walking and me pockets are bulging when I get home. There's lots of things I can add to the weaving, like beads, feathers, ribbons, shells, pieces of rope, rushes and dried flowers; I've tried them all. And I've made a fair bit of money. I'm going to try dyeing too." She went over to the windowsill and picked up a jar, took off the top and offered it to Rose.

"Smell it," she demanded.

Rose didn't need to go near it; she could smell it from where she was standing. The stench coming from the jar was repulsive, and she retched.

"Ugh! What is that?" she asked, using her handkerchief to dab at her streaming eyes.

"Woad. The plants grow wild, like weeds."

"What colour is it meant to be?"

"Blue. And this," Mary said, selecting a dried plant, "is alkanet, which is a bit boring really because it goes grey. From sumac I get brown. Walnut shells make tan. Lots of dyes don't work; they just come out brown and grey. I don't know why. Must be sommat I ain't doing right, but I'll keep practising. I can make yellow from marigolds, onions and nettle, even teasles, which are so good for brushing up the pile on cloth. Green comes from elder and foxgloves, and red from the root of meadowsweet. It's fun. You should try it."

"What are you going to do with the dyes?"

"Make rugs and cushions and then sell them. If anything's left over, I'll keep it to make the house pretty. I sold a wall hanging I made because I needed money to pay for flax seed."

"Come and see this," Mary said, dragging Rose over to a large wooden table, which looked suspiciously as if it had been made from several old weaving looms.

"The children have been making these." She lifted a cloth and uncovered piles of brightly coloured belts, bracelets, sashes and hair decorations. "Aren't they pretty? They're made by tablet and finger weaving. I'll show you how when I've got the time. It's a bit like making rope, but the children knot the end and tie it to the door knob." She grinned. "That's why we haven't any. Most of them's fallen off."

She picked up a piece of braid and put it around Rose's neck. "Look how it brightens up your dress. I'll be able to sell a lot of those."

Rose was puzzled. They'd been away for two weeks. How long had Mary been home, and where had Nancy been whilst she was entertaining the children? It wasn't that she minded, of course, but what had been going on at the twine works while Mary was 'decorating'? She had been behaving very oddly.

"How is business?" she asked brightly.

"Fine."

"And the workers?"

"Fine."

There was a pause, and then Mary said, "It was just to keep the children happy. Nancy went off home to visit her boyfriend for a few days, so I said I'd look after them 'til she came back."

"I hope they weren't too much for you."

"Oh no. It was fun."

"Who's been doing the spinning, whilst you've been working in here?" As soon as she had asked the question, Rose realised she should never have asked it.

Mary whipped around to face her, her eyes flashing with anger. "That's nothing to do with you," she snapped. "You should be grateful that I looked after your child. If you must know, a close friend from the village helped me out, and anyway, I'm supposed to be away resting while you've been gallivanting with my son."

"You know full well I went with Tom to Bridport to help him," Rose said, her cheeks reddening with embarrassment, realising too late that she had badly upset the woman she had hoped to make her friend. "We've learned a lot, and with your help we would like to put our ideas into practice," she said humbly, trying to rescue herself.

"Well, you're not going to get it if you talk to me like that."

She hadn't expected that reaction. Oh dear! How could she make her see that she only wanted to help? Her moods were strange, too. She hadn't know her long, but... She put her head in her hands and closed her eyes.

Mary put out her hand and stroked her hair. "Whatever's the matter, Rose? I'm annoyed with you, but I didn't expect you to take it to heart..."

Rose looked up. "It isn't just that."

"What then?"

"I can't read or write," she whispered. "I'm too ashamed to tell Tom, but I won't be any use to him if I can't help with the accounts, or write letters."

"It's nice to know you're taking this seriously," Mary said briskly. "Why don't you ask Bess to help you; she was a governess not so long ago. She taught me all I know, and I'm sure between us we'll manage."

Rose brightened considerably when Tom entered the room.

"I've been thinking," he said. "Why don't we give demonstrations? Show people what we do. Invite everyone in the village. Tell them why we have to make an effort to help our country. Some people may prefer to join one of the voluntary defence units, or the Navy, but others can learn to spin, to sew, or make twine. What do you think?"

"How many workers do you think we'll need then, Tom?" Mary said.

"As many outworkers as we can find; and then I shall need a couple of rooms upstairs in the cottage cleared to make a new workroom."

"Alter the bedrooms? Where will we sleep?"

"In one of the outhouses. We can make it nice and comfortable, and by the winter I hope we'll have made enough money to build a new workroom, and then we can claim back our bedrooms.

Mary folded her arms and shook her head. "It'll never work. There isn't enough time. And anyway, who will do all the work whilst we're training?"

"We'll manage, because we have to." Tom scratched his head, wondering what to do. "We need to make money so that we can afford to buy land, labour, seed, machinery, and eventually the new workroom, and that means we need labourers to keep working while we train more people. Then we must try to get all the other mill owners to work with us. I am desperately serious about this, mother, for how else is our country to survive? The Navy needs our help. There is a terrific amount of canvas to be made; of course it won't all come from the southwest, but each ship needs nearly four acres of canvas, so you can imagine how much cloth a fleet of about twenty ships will use. Eventually women will take the place of men, as men will no doubt soon be going to fight, but we will have no young children. I will not exploit them, whatever the cost.

"So when do we start?" Rose asked anxiously. "And who will do the training?"

Tom looked at his mother, and after a few moments thought, she nodded her head.

"Well, ladies," he said, smiling. "It would seem that we are all set to go, so I would suggest that I make up some leaflets, and when we have received replies to them we'll be in business.

Chapter 13

Tom received about forty replies from the village folk, and decided to split them up, according to experience, into four divisions of ten people. Men, women, and older children had volunteered for the training, and Tom, Mary, Rose, and Joshua, one of the ropeworkers, took a group each.

Joshua took his group away to the ropewalk, and Mary held a business class at her kitchen table, where various men and women would learn to do the paperwork, raise and pay invoices, write letters and do the accounts. Rose would teach weaving, spinning, and then all the other processes that were part of producing the cloth. Tom would show them how to stitch and make up the sails.

Most of the younger women had chosen to do the weaving, so Rose led them to the bottom of the spinning shed, and sat each of them in front of an empty loom, handing them a bundle of threads to work with.

"I will try to remember your names," she said, "but please forgive me if I sometimes get them wrong. My name is Rose, and today I will show you how to weave. How many of you have done weaving before?"

Three hands shot up.

"Right then. I want you three to come to the front. You can help me teach the others."

Two girls and one middle aged woman came forward.

"Lily, Elizabeth, and Edith. All of you should know what you are doing as I have taught you all. Perhaps you would like to take two ladies each; I will teach the others. But first, I should like the experts to demonstrate, and the others can watch."

Rose and the three women sat down at the looms, and the rest of them crowded around. Twenty minutes later, they were ready to start.

"There's no need to hurry," said Rose. "I want you to get it right. Everyone. Show me your hands."

Ten pairs of hands were dutifully held out in front of her, palms upwards.

"Excellent. I see that you have washed them. Now, how about your nails?"

Ten pairs of nails were displayed.

"Good. All beautifully clean. I am impressed. Well done. I hope you remember to check them every day before you come to work. You will not be allowed to work on my looms until you have washed your hands under the pump. Understood?"

Ten heads nodded in agreement.

"Teachers. Perhaps you would show your students how to position the warp threads lengthwise on the loom, and I will show mine. The threads that are woven across it are the weft. Do you understand?"

Diligent fingers picked up the threads and the students allowed the trainers to help them arrange the threads on the loom.

Rose walked along the two rows of women checking their work.

"Excellent. Now we pass the thread back and forth, through the warp to form the weft, or the picks. Do a little for me so that I can see you do it."

The students duly obeyed.

"Well done. You all managed that very well." She handed out more threads. "See how much you can do before we take a break. Thank you, ladies."

Tom put together a few sewing palms, some hooks, a few needles and various sizes of twine before calling Onesiphorous, Harry, John, Albert, William, Joseph, Fred,

George, Zach and Charlie upstairs to the spare bedroom, where various shapes of canvas had been set out around the room. Even though it was September, the room was dark, and the candles set about the room gave little light. In the new workroom, thought Tom, wide windows would be especially built into the walls so that the sail makers could take advantage of every vestige of light that came into the room, so that they could work late into the evening.

He lit the lanterns to chase away the shadows, then sat down on a bench opposite his students.

"You will see various pieces of sail spread around the room, and it is our job to sew them together. In time, you will come to know the name of each sail, and where it fits onto a ship, and what it is for. The pieces of cloth over by the window have been cut into the shape of a mainsail. Come on over and take a look."

The men clustered around the piece of cloth, and watched while Tom overlapped two pieces of canvas. "You must make sure that the overlap is the same as the width of the seam, for which we use a flat stitch."

He demonstrated, slipping the needle through the canvas, making five stitches to the inch. "This thread is quadrupled, or doubled over twice," he said, making sure that they could see. "I am using a bench hook, and please note, that I am wearing a sewing palm so that my hands don't become riddled with holes."

He unwrapped a piece of cloth to reveal several steel needles, and picked out one that was round in shape from the eye to halfway down its length, the sides becoming triangular and meeting in a point.

"You will use one of these for the round edges of the sail." He held up another needle. "This is for a flat seam using single thread. Your twine must be thicker than the threads of the canvas, but we'll do that later. That big one is a bolt needle, and can take between ten and twelve threads.

The next size is a grommet, for four threads, and this last one, the heading needle, will take two, three or four threads. Handle them, gentlemen, carefully now, and feel the shape of them."

"Now, if the seam is in the middle of a sail, that is, the bight or the bend of the sail, it must be doubled towards you over your knee when sewing, like this," he said, demonstrating again, "but I'll help you when we come to it." He stood up.

"Gentlemen. Would you like to have a go at sewing a seam? Don't forget the sewing palms." He indicated the pile and left the men to help themselves, but Onesiphorous wandered away without one.

Joseph and Harry worked quickly, as they were used to the work. Onesiphorous and Albert, however, were struggling with the weight of the cloth.

"I've cut me finger," moaned Onesiphorous. "There's blood all over it now."

"Use your palm," advised Tom, and threw him one from the pile.

Onesiphorous put his hand through the leather bracelet and his thumb through the hole.

"Will everyone watch how Onesiphorous does it? Notice, too, the brass disc in the centre of the palm. That is the seaming eye. You will see that it is fastened by lugs, and criss-crossed by raised lines so that the needle won't jump out when you're using it. "

He handed Onesiphorous a pot of liquid. "This is the tallow where you will dip your needles to stop them slipping. Normally it is kept in a grease horn, but we haven't one. That blood needs to be washed off, Onesiphorous, or it will go all over the sail."

"It's blooming hard to push the needle through, even with the palm on," moaned Albert. "I need a hammer to knock it in, but then I'd probably miss and hit me knee."

This is ridiculous, he thought. "Don't be such a baby, Albert," he said with a sigh. "Let's look at what you've done."

But he was surprised. "That's not bad. Not bad at all," he said, looking up at him. "What was all the fuss about? You've done a brilliant job."

"How many stitches should we do?" asked William. "I've done one so far."

"There should be two rows of stitches, side by side. The underneath cloth is pricked twice by the needle, but the top piece is only pricked once at the very edge of the cloth. The stitches are quite small, as you can see from my work. Yours are a bit big, William, but as this is a practice it doesn't matter."

For the next hour everyone worked industriously, joining the strips together, until gradually the sail started to take shape. After a while, Tom handed around bread, cheese and mugs of milk and they had a rest.

"Now I'll show you how to make the hem."

Tom went over to a wooden box and selected a piece of twine. "Hemming is also known as tabling, and it's sewn around the whole sail," he said, taking the needle and inserting it into the folded cloth, showing them how to form a line of neat stitches.

"Look at the head of the sail. Can you see that it's wider? That's how it should look when you've finished. "Now, the edge of the tabling is tucked under on the inside edge and sewn down, and this seam is called a sticking seam. And there you are! You've finished the first part!"

Tom fetched some strips of canvas from the box. "The sail is strengthened by sewing these strips down the whole drop of the sail on either side, over the top of the tabling. So please concentrate, and I'll show you how to do it."

So for the rest of the day Tom's team learnt how to make sails, until at seven o' clock, Onesiphorous stood up and stretched.

"I've had enough of this, " he said, and yawned. "I don't know about anyone else, but I'm ready for me tea. Me eyes are going crooked with all this sewing."

"Be patient for a while longer," begged Tom. "We've nearly finished. Look at Harry and Joseph. They've done really well."

"They've done it afore," moaned Onesiphorous. "I must 'ave been a babe in me cradle when Joseph was making his first sail."

"Don't be such a misery," said William. "You should be grateful for Tom for being so patient with you. I'd have drowned you in the river long afore."

"Stop quarrelling," pleaded Tom. "You're doing fine, all of you."

For a while they worked quietly, each thinking their own thoughts as their needles dipped in and out of the material as they tried to concentrate on the task.

"Finally, the leech ropes have to be sewn on, just above the lower corner, or the clew," Tom explained. "Then the bolt rope is sewn to the front of the sail, and a cringle is made at the clew."

"A cringle is made at the clew?" echoed Onesiphorous, his voice rising in disbelief. "I speak English, Thomas, not this stupid foreign language. I'm going home for my dinner, and surely I deserve a gallon of cider after all I've been through this afternoon."

"I tell you what, if you don't be quiet, Onesiphorous," Harry said, "I will personally wrap you up in that blessed sail and suffocate you with it. You ain't done nothing but moan. If I were you, Tom, I'd have flung him out ages ago."

"I don't think I like your manner," Onesiphorous said, bunching his fists and taking a swing at Harry, but missing him entirely. "I don't have to put up with you, or the damned carry on with this stupid business."

"No you don't," Harry agreed, "and if I were you I'd leave before you do something you'll be sorry for."

"I ain't sorry for nothing," shouted Onesiphorous. "And especially I'm not sorry for knocking your head off."

Tom had heard and seen enough, and now he came to stand between the two angry men, ducking Onesiphorous's fist as it tried to connect with Harry's chin. "That will do, gentlemen," he said, seizing Onesiphorous's hand and removing the sewing palm, which he was using as a weapon. "I think it would a good idea if both of you went home and cooled down. If I had a bucket of water I'd throw it over the pair of you."

But Harry's temper had risen out of control and he was determined not to leave until he had delivered his final insult.

"At least I don't drink cider until it's coming out of me ears." He held up his fists threateningly, his feet moving deftly as he pranced round Onesiphorous, goading him to a fight. "Come on then, slobberguts. Let's see what you're made of. Shake them old bones o' yours and hit me. Go on," he goaded. "Hit me, knock me down."

"Right. You asked for it," muttered Onesiphorous, thrusting out an arm vaguely in Harry's direction, but his punch landed on Tom's chin, knocking him down. Undaunted, Harry put down his head and charged at Onesiphorous like an angry bull, pushing him against a wall, and Onesiphorous retaliated by kicking out with his feet.

Harry squealed and then retreated, holding his hands in front of his crotch.

"You bastard," he shouted. "I'll teach you to damage me privates. Just as well for you I've had all me children.

"There ain't no point damaging your brain cos you ain't got one," Onesiphorous said spitefully, pushing Harry backwards with his hands until the older sailmaker caught his foot in one of the boltropes and fell over.

Tom scrambled to his feet, caught Onesiphorous by the arm and dragged him to the doorway and put him outside.

Onesiphorous yelled and banged about in the passageway, until Tom stepped outside to speak to him.

"Go away, Onesiphorous, and don't come back," he said quietly, shutting the door behind him.

"I've been wanting to do that for years," Joseph said in admiration. "That man gives me a headache."

"He deserved it, " Tom said shortly. "We'll do more tomorrow. The light has gone, so we'll stop there. Thank you for coming, and I'll see you back here at six o'clock in the morning."

Tom tidied away the loose materials, leaving the pieces of sail in place, then snuffed out the lanterns before leaving the room. As he made his way down the stairs he reflected on the day's events. It was difficult to know how much the men had understood, but their attempts at sewing were admirable, apart from Onesiphorous, who would never change. Whether he would make a good employee was another matter; from village gossip he had learned that he spent most of his time drunk, and several hours lying in ditches.

He sat on the bottom step, rested his elbows on his knees, put his head in his hands, and was soon deep in thought. A moment of self-doubt had settled upon him, and he started examining his motives.

Was he being selfish expecting everyone to aid his ambition? Rose seemed to be happy about her new role, but his mother wasn't so sure. Was he being fair to her? Was he being too domineering, pushing everyone to their limits to achieve his dream? Perhaps he had lost sight of something more important, the time to allow people to be with the ones they loved.

But he had to be realistic. They were short of time. There was a war looming and he needed labourers who could do their job well. It was important to make sure that enough men were trained to work in the trade, so the sooner he arranged to meet some of the local mill owners to discuss the situation the better.

However, before he was able to make his first appointment, he was called up to serve on the Victory.

Chapter 14

Rose walked along South Street, past the little houses built for the workers at Viney Bridge Mills at Crewkerne, where the women weavers sat outside on stools, heads down as they worked industriously at their looms. Half a hour before she had nervously anticipated a meeting with Samuel Sparks, one of the partners of the Viney Bridge Mills, specialists in the spinning of flax and the weaving of webbing.

They did not look up as she passed, or notice the jubilant smile that played about her lips. After a while she did a little skip and a jump; she had done Tom proud, and she was sublimely happy.

At first, she had struggled to make Mr Sparks understand the purpose of their meeting, and then when she did, she had had to confirm that the rumour spread by Squire Seymour was true, but that it had been based on spite and greed.

Mr Sparks had had several disagreements with the squire, and fully understood her position, and after that it had not taken her long to satisfy him that his mill would benefit from a joint venture with other mills in his district. Patiently she had explained about the warehouse, the loan of a boat to export their goods, and the mutual advantages of sharing a carrier. She had needed him to understand that this was not about competition, but for the preservation of their country.

Mr Sparks had consulted his partner, Mr Bartholemew Gidley, who expressed an interest in her suggestion, and eventually she had been able to convince Mr Sparks to add their names to the 'list' of other 'prominent' factories and contribute the skills of their workforce and use of their mill to provide a continuous supply of goods for the British Navy.

The Viney Bridge Mill utilised the shallow water from the river Parrett tributary to drive the mill, which was ideally situated on the north to south routes leading to the Dorset ports, and the London to Exeter road. Apart from being in a good position to use the warehouse at Bridport, canvas could be sent either by sea to Portsmouth and to other parts of the country, or by road to London by Russell's Carriers, and raw materials could be returned from London as necessary.

She had noted, too, that labourers at the mill were paid by tokens, which were then redeemed at a bank in town that had been set up by Samuel Sparks himself, an idea that she tucked away in her mind for later, when she could discuss it with Tom.

The following day she approached Richard Hayward of Bridge House at West Chinnock with the same request, and then the Randall family more locally at West Coker, each time coming away with a favourable reply.

Now Rose was left with the dilemma of understanding the huge ledgers that Tom's father James kept in the small office at the back of the cottage.

Who could help her? Swiftly she ran through a mental list of contacts, at last settling upon ex-governess Aunt Bess from East Coker. Tom had talked about her many times.

He had told her that Bess wanted him to do well, and felt that she had a duty to do the right thing by his mother. But this particular lady had connections with a certain Viscount and a Captain, who had suggested that they in turn might be able to speak to the Naval Inspector. Now. How could she convince this lady that she was a decent person, who was doing her best to maintain Tom's business whilst he was away, and had every intention of working with his mother to improve the conditions at the ropeworks? What's more she would tell her that she needed help with the accounting side of the business, as now that Tom had gone, his mother would not be able to manage on her own.

She must try to be businesslike, and to dress accordingly. The new yellow pelisse and the cream silk would do nicely, for she needed to look respectable if she was to approach this lady, and to mind her manners. She should try to speak in more cultured tones, for whatever would the lady think of her broad Somerset accent? She had heard that Bess approved of the new way of thinking, favouring the entrepreneur, and was undeniably a monarchist; in fact, she was aware of the general opinion she was a snob, and she hated snobs. Nevertheless, if this snob had money and influence, then she was prepared to do whatever it took to impress her. Suddenly she grinned, and her eyes twinkled. Whatever would Tom think if he knew her thoughts? That he wouldn't care at all she was quite convinced.

Bess received her with a frown and compressed lips, unaware of Rose's determination for her plan to succeed.

"I'm aware we haven't met, Miss Hill, but I do assure you that I love Tom, and have no wish to harm him, his business, or his mother, come to that. I have every intention of taking care of the business in his absence; only last week I met several businessmen who agreed to form an association with us to ensure that our goods would reach their intended destination faster. And by sharing a carrier we will be able to dispatch extra merchandise to where it is needed most."

"Hmm. The wars with the French. Tom's gone, then." Bess poured hot water into the teapot and left it to brew.

Rose looked at her hopefully. "I think a battle is inevitable. Have you heard anything?

"You mean, from my acquaintances? No. I can't say that I have. But I dare say I shall hear from them soon. Anyway."

Bess poured the tea and sat down opposite Rose across the kitchen table. "You haven't come to see me just to ask me that." Her eyes narrowed and seemed to look straight through her. "What have you really come for, Mrs Howard?"

"Help. And advice, if you would be so kind."

"Why?"

"Because I want to help and I don't know how."

"You seem an intelligent woman. I should have thought you would be full of ideas."

"I am. I can read and write a little, but I know nothing about figures and accounts. Mary has taught some of the labourers how to do it, and I feel so stupid. I know that you were once a governess…"

"Governesses look after children, not money."

"But surely…"

To her surprise Bess smiled. "As it happens I can do accounts. I used to help my brother when he lived with me. And as you seem to be committed to this business I shall be happy to show you."

"I don't suppose you could mention our plans to your … er… acquaintances?" Rose asked boldly. "Tom told me that they were interested in our canvas, and mentioned a certain Naval Inspector?"

"You don't waste time, do you, young lady. " Bess picked up Rose's reticule from the floor and handed it to her. "That's pretty," she said. "I should have thought you would have preferred something a little … plainer."

Rose glanced at her silk hand-embroidered bag and frowned. "Why's that, Miss Hill?"

"Well, I would have thought you a practical person, Mrs Howard, not given to fanciful things."

Rose smiled. "My daughter is a creative child, and she has taught me to decorate the simplest and cheapest of my possessions. "

"I must say that I have revised my opinion of you." Bess said. "You are such a flexible soul. I like people who know what they want and go all out to get it, but you are imaginative, too. I shall be delighted to mention your suggestion to Alex and Samuel, and I'm sure they'll do all they can do to help." Her voice softened.

"How are you coping with Tom's absence, my dear? It must be hard not knowing how or even where he is."

"It's kind of you to ask," replied Rose. "I have to admit it's not easy. I am so fond of him."

She drained her cup, set it down on the table, then arose and made her way to the door. Abruptly she turned and held out her hand. "You have been more than helpful, Miss Hill, and I am very grateful. The only thing left to do is to persuade Farmer Brown to rent us some land, and I shall visit him directly I arrive home. We need a good yield of flax to accomplish the plans that I have for a new workshop, and now that we have trained labourers to help I hope it won't take us too long to build it. We have a lot of work to do, and the sooner we start the better."

Bess shook Rose's hand. "I wish you all the best, Mrs Howard. Naturally, I shall require a fee for my work. I cannot feed and clothe myself on fresh air. Thank you for coming, and I shall look forward to seeing you shortly."

And then, to Rose's surprise, she winked.

Her feet barely touched the ground as she walked home. It was the end of summer; the cornfields had been stripped, and the oxen had ploughed brown furrows into the land. In the orchards the apples were ripening, and hazel nuts were forming in the hedgerows. She was alone with her thoughts, but whilst many of them focussed upon the business, she realised how badly she missed Tom. The two of them had grown closer during the too short weeks before he left, and now she wished he were here to share her successes and plans for the future. He would have been so pleased that she and Bess now understood each other, but whilst she and Mary did not always see eye to eye, they would have to try to work together.

But once Emily had been put to bed in her little house, even familiar noises unsettled her and made her jump; her daughter's gentle snoring mingled with the soft wind soughing through the thatch, and in the distance the wood pigeons cooed, distracting her now and then with the clatter of their wings when they were disturbed, perhaps by the barking of a dog or the braying of an ox. But most of all she missed being able to talk to Tom about everyday things, and the feeling of safety his presence gave her.

Rose's lack of financial knowledge proved to be limiting; she was trying to work out how much her cloth would be worth, and every time she tried the figure grew too large and she gave up.

"Two shillings and two pence per yard for first quality, times five thousand bolts," Mary said, and wrote the answer in the little book she always carried with her

Bess's lessons were helping, but she didn't find figures easy. They needed new machinery, more seed, more looms, and most of all she needed to pay Farmer Brown, who had agreed to rent her the land she needed in return for a reasonable rent, but whenever she needed money she had to ask Mary for it, and she so wanted to be independent The business was doing well, but not well enough. She was working sixteen hours a day, and Emily was growing bored with playing with Ben.

Her daughter needed something else; too young for labouring, she had told her mother that she wanted to learn how to read and write. Rose had heard of a Dame's school starting up locally, and she thought it about time she sent Emily. Ben could go too, if he wanted. She was his minder now, for Tom had given her sole charge, which naturally upset Mary, but not everything in this world was perfect.

164

She became friendly with Elizabeth, one of the older labourers who had no children of her own, and they sat quietly talking in her living room most evenings. They were becoming increasingly dependant on one another as they helped to turn out sailcloth by day, sharing experiences as a new kind of empathy formed between them. Elizabeth could read and write, so between them they managed to make up a sheaf of leaflets to be sent out with the canvas that was sent by Russell's Carriers, advertising the fact that they would also supply other merchandise. Jim Gilbert was not the only mill owner to expand his trade.

The weeks passed peacefully, apart from one Tuesday when she and Elizabeth nearly caused an outbreak of hysteria in the workroom. To give a good shiny finish to the twine, the two women had tipped clear turpentine and hog's lard into the beeswax melting in a large copper pot over the fire.

They hesitated, unsure how to proceed.

"Have you seen how Tom used to do it?" Rose giggled, slightly tipsy from several glasses of mead.

"Never." Elizabeth eyed the greasy, smelly mixture with distaste. "I don't fancy touching it, do you?"

"Can't stare at it all day, can we?" replied Rose. "The twine won't coat itself, will it?"

"I'll count to five, then we'll do it together."

"Five."

Taking deep breaths, the two women rolled up their sleeves, threw the twine into the pot, closed their eyes and plunged their arms up to the armpits into the gruesome mixture, smearing it over the twine time after time to build up a hard shiny coat.

But they had forgotten the mountains of dust and fluff that had accumulated under the machines, and now the messy liquid was attracting the grey dust balls that were constantly in their mouths and up their noses. Gradually, each layer of grease obtained a further layer of fluff, until, unable to remove it, they wandered through the workroom like a couple of woolly goats.

"My God," shouted Mrs Cooper, running to the door "We've got creatures from hell in here. I'm going home to my Henry."

"Not much difference between 'em," muttered Jem Cuthbert, his cheeks bulging with lumps of tobacco.

"Best fetch Farmer Brown from his milking," he said.

"Mebbe he'll get his shears out," laughed Becky Sharp, a new starter, like Jem and Mrs Cooper. "Fancy a new coat for the winter, anyone?"

Chapter 15

Then came the day of the letter from the Naval Inspector, Jack Hayward, who was a personal friend of the Hood family. He would, he wrote, be visiting the following week, and, having been told about the excellent quality of the cloth, was looking forward to meeting the ladies who helped to produce it.

In a fever of excitement Mary and Rose issued frenzied orders to the workers to ensure they were tidy and wearing their caps, and that the new workroom was clean and well swept.

The men at the retting pond and ropeworks were seen to be amazingly busy and well organised, and had cleared the mud from the work area as it was the first place to be seen when the inspector walked down the path.

As he stepped from his curricle Rose perceived that Jack Hayward was a tall, good-looking man, about thirty years old, with a cheeky glint in his merry blue eyes and a smile the length of the rope walk. His brown hair was thick and luxuriant, his beard curled beautifully around his ears, and when he parted his lips in a friendly smile his teeth gleamed, his appreciative glance taking in Rose's slim waist and ankles, and it was at this point that Rose became aware that he was probably a rogue.

Knowing that although she was no classic beauty, but passably attractive, Rose preened herself in front of him like a peacock, playing with the mahogany ringlets that framed her heart-shaped face, batting her eyelashes mischievously and biting her lips to redden them to show him that here was a lady prepared to flirt with an attractive man, and ready to make a good impression upon him, 'though unfortunately not for the reasons he would have wished.

His full attention was now upon her, for poor Mary, with her lank grey hair, sallow complexion and thickening figure stood no chance, and remained in the background, for all he knew the mother of this very desirable woman. What he did not know, however, was that Mary was seething with anger as she watched her son's girl throwing herself at him, without realising that it was all for show.

He held out his hand and Rose took it, curtseying low as he kissed it.

"Pleased to meet you, sir," she smiled.

"Likewise," replied the Naval Inspector, smiling happily as she led him unsuspectingly towards the extraction of an order for several hundred bolts of cloth for his battleships.

"I have received an exceptionally good report from those wonderful gentlemen, Alexander Viscount Hood and Captain Hood, newly promoted to Commodore, I believe. Coker grass bleached canvas cannot be equalled by any foreign export." He beamed widely. "I have come to see the quality for myself, and if it is good enough I have been authorised to order a suit of sails for a ship of each rate, at least, to start with."

His eyes seemed unable to leave her face, his fascination for her almost causing her to swoon under such flattering attention. "In fact," he continued, "the First Lord of the Admiralty has asked for it especially. Coker canvas is of the best kind, and very much in demand. If you would be good enough to show me around your workroom and then, if everything is satisfactory, I am sure some business can be done this afternoon." He coughed, politely shielding his mouth with his hand. And then he added, "double thread, of course?"

"Of course," Rose replied seriously. "Nothing else."

As she luxuriated in her sensual experience, Rose felt a certain satisfaction that she was actually dallying with an inspector of the Navy. He was to be encouraged, for with his help they could acquire more orders, which in turn could lead to perhaps several new workshops with more machinery and extra workers. Her ambition knew no bounds, her confidence soared. They could do it, of course they could. But at the same time, she knew that without Bess, it would not have been possible at all.

Rose approached the inspector as he was examining a pile of newly woven cloth, and she watched as he checked it for durability and strength, stability and ability to soak up water. Finally, Mr Hayward looked up, and she was delighted to see that he was beaming again.

"Excellent stuff, Mrs Howard. Given that flax is difficult to spin finely due to its coarse thread, you have succeeded very well. I am impressed. The problem we have at the moment is dampness and mildew, due to heavy gales in the Gulf of Lyons, and the use of your sailcloth is highly desirable. I see this cloth has fewer threads and a more open weave, and therefore a greater porosity than a cloth of the same weight per square yard. It also has a low stretch factor. Excellent! Excellent. I shall have no problem recommending that the Navy order five thousand bolts at two shillings and sixpence a yard. How soon would you have that amount ready, do you think?"

Rose was blushing furiously from the praise being heaped upon her, her fuddled mind finding it impossible to estimate a date when goods could be delivered to Bridport Dock.

"I…er…think…In fact, Mr Hayward," she said positively, "I can be certain that your order will be completed by the twenty-fifth of this month, if that is acceptable?" Rose's heart was beating so rapidly she thought she would faint, but it would not do to fall at Jack

Hayward's feet. At the last minute her mind had cleared and she had given him a date she thought achievable. Everything seemed to be happening at once, but she was loving every minute of it.

"We need more people such as yourself," Jack Hayward said as he walked around the workroom, his eyes missing nothing. "Village industries are flourishing now, and if you become prosperous you will be able to pay your workers bonuses. Up until now, many large employing farmers have not paid fair wages, and both the poor rate and enclosures are taking their toll. It is a very unfair system, Mrs Howard, and I for one am awaiting a change. I am certain that you are a moral person, and do not treat your workers in such a fashion. Times are hard enough. We do not need to make them worse."

"Oh, how I do agree, Mr Hayward," she simpered. "As you rightly suspect, we pay our workers a living wage, and any profits are ploughed back in." She would say anything he wanted to hear. It wasn't that she wouldn't, it was more that she couldn't pay her workers a decent wage, but he didn't need to know that.

Jack Hayward offered his hand to seal the deal, and Rose shook it eagerly, her respect showing in the way she inclined her head towards him. She was gratified by the way his appreciative glance swept over her and she smiled seductively.

"Thank you for coming, Mr Hayward, and for the order you have placed with us. I am sure you will be delighted with our service, as we will give your order our best attention.

"And I trust we shall meet again very soon."

The Naval Inspector smiled and Rose's knees trembled. He was indeed a very attractive man. She wondered briefly whether he had a wife, but she would never have pursued him. To have an affair with an attractive officer from the

Navy was an appealing proposition, but for one thing he had probably won the respect of several ladies, and for another, Tom had won her heart and she would never risk losing him. And besides, she was doing this so that she and Tom could serve the country they loved and the great Nelson, for whom they both had the greatest of respect.

Minutes later Rose watched Jack Hayward pass through the garden gate from behind the safety of her bedroom curtains, circle the retting pond and pass the time of day with the ropeworkers before he doffed his hat, climbed into the waiting curricle and disappeared from view around the bend in the stream.

Mary was overawed by her achievement. "You've done it," she gasped, her eyes bright in her pale face. But then her brow creased in a frown.

"What worries me, Rose, is where are we going to find the machines to spin all that yarn, and is our new workroom big enough?"

And that was something that concerned Rose, too.

At the end of July, Villeneuve returned from the Caribbean, but a British squadron was lying in wait off Finisterre on the Brittany coast. Lord Byron of the Navy Board had drawn forces from the blockading fleets on the Atlantic coasts of France and Spain and massed them under Calder's command. Villeneuve blocked his move north, but lost two of his ships, retreating to the Port of Corunna in northern Spain.

In a vain attempt to reach the Channel, Villeneuve spotted a British battleship and frigate, but he was informed by a passing Danish merchant ship that they were part of a powerful squadron, when in reality, they were alone. Believing this to be true, Villeneuve turned south for Cadiz, his invasion plan ruined. As an experienced sailor, he knew what it meant to be caught by the British in open sea, and now he resigned himself to his fate. He was in an impossible position; his tormentor was out at sea; nervously he awaited orders from Napoleon.

A few days later, Villeneuve arrived at Vigo, reaching Ferrol on the first of August. Ten days later, Nelson had been expecting him to arrive at the Bay of Biscay, but he had not yet arrived. However, on the thirteenth he left Ferrol with twenty-eight ships of the line.

On the thirtieth of August, eighteen hundred and five, Pierre Villeneuve had been waiting off the mouth of Cadiz Harbour for the Spanish ships to join his fleet, presuming that Lord Nelson's fleet would pursue them. He had hoped that his ships would slip past Nelson, but now he felt desperate; having no confidence in either his men or his ships he was forced to take refuge in Cadiz, where Vice Admiral Collingwood was waiting with the British fleet, watching him.

Nelson had briefly returned home to his mistress, Emma Hamilton, for a rest, but on the thirteenth of September he left Morton in Norfolk and travelled by coach to Portsmouth through the night, where a longboat was waiting to take him to the Victory. He was held in great esteem by the adoring crowds who had mobbed and cheered him as his boat pulled away from the docks, and on the twenty-ninth of September, his forty-seventh birthday, he was reunited with the men on board his ship.

Nelson was a small man, but his frail body belied inner strengths; he had a knack for inspiring his officers and fellow seamen, whom he understood and filled with a sense of purpose, whilst at the same time he was a clever man, a tactical, quick thinker.

Nelson had withdrawn fifty miles offshore from Cadiz to entice out the Combined Fleet, whilst a cordon of lookout ships between the port and the fleet reported their movements.

The seventeen thousand men of the fleet gave Nelson a rapturous welcome. He welcomed his officers on board the Victory and laid before them his plan of action.

Thomas Freemantle, commanding the Neptune, together with the other fourteen Captains, dined with him on his forty-seventh birthday around a table full of polished silver and gleaming mahogany, where he announced that if he should die, he wished to be buried in St Paul's Cathedral.

The French fleet started to come out of port on the nineteenth of October, but progress was slow, owing to lack of wind. By the next day the British fleet were close to the mouth of the Straits, but the weather was foul. In the distance, the sea mist occasionally cleared so that the towering cliffs of Cape Trafalgar could be seen, but the Combined Fleet of the French and Spanish were due north, out of sight of the British. As the day wore on the mists began to clear and the wind that had been slowing down the enemy fleet shifted, and they came out of port.

Nelson was determined not to lose sight of them again, and signalled to the two ships that had recently joined them to paint the hoops of their masts yellow, like the rest of his fleet, distinguishing them from the black hoops of the enemy; and to burn two blue lights together, every hour, so that they could be seen more easily, and to fire three guns in succession every hour.

On Monday the twenty-first of October the mists cleared at dawn, a drum tattoo called the men to their quarters, the sound echoing across the anchorage, and each ship hoisted her colours. Cape Trafalgar was twenty-one miles away, almost due east. The line was divided; Nelson's Victory headed one column of ships, Collingwood's Sovereign the other. They sailed at the centre and rear of the enemy line with the intention of bringing the British ships into close action and to cut off the van of the

Combined Fleet. Twenty-seven ships of the line were running before a light onshore wind, the enemy's thirty-three ships forming a crescent, Villeneuve taking his ships around to head back to Cadiz.

And on the lower gun deck of the Victory, tense and anxious, the crew waited for the battle to begin.

The hum of activity grew louder as Rose reached the top of the stairs, and when she opened the door to the new workroom the heat nearly knocked her backwards.

"I've opened all the windows," shouted Mary over the noise of the looms. "The heat is unbearable."

"It's a pity the workers can't work outside," said Rose, loudly. "It's hard to breathe in here."

The heat was certainly overpowering, thought Rose, but the rancid smell of perspiration mingled with the familiar rankness of vegetable fibre made it worse. It was a different kind of pungency from that at the mill, for there, the machines had smelled of oil, and grease clung to the workers' feet and yellowed their faces.

Specks of fibre and dust hung in a haze above the spinners and weavers, and they had bundled their hair into caps to protect them from it. The noise here was bad, but Rose remembered that in Gilbert's mill the machines with their pulsating humming belts and constantly running wheels were even more deafening.

Long shafts of sunlight fell on four rows of women as they spun flax at their spinning wheels, whilst the weavers turned the thread into sailcloth on their looms.

She went over to speak to a bewhiskered old man who was dressing a line of fibre ready for hand spinning. She watched as Joseph took a strick of rough fibre by the head-ends, spread out the root end, and by lashing the tips on the heckle pulled the fibres through the teeth. He repeated the action several times before he was satisfied, then reversed the strick and did it again. He picked up a five inch heckle with more closely set teeth and repeated the action once more.

"How are you, Joseph? Has your daughter had that grandchild of yours yet? Seems to me she's been pregnant for a year."

"This new workroom is grand, Mrs Howard. 'Tis a pleasure to work for you. And thanks for asking about Beth. She won't be long now. Missus is making her scrub all the floors, but nothing have happened yet."

"Well, let me know when it does. Oh yes, I nearly forgot. I've heard that the Burton mill is using the new power loom recently invented by Cartwright. It's faster than anything we own, and as soon as we can afford it, it'll be yours. But with that, the flax has to be drawn out into slivers and twisted, ready for the machine. It will be twice as fine. D'you know," she said eagerly, "an average machine count is one hundred and fifty skeins of three hundred yards each to a pound. Clever, isn't it?"

"It's a wonder what these contraptions can do, ain't it, miss? Anything that quickens up the procedure is fine with me. The more we turn out the better for everyone. That's what I say."

"I quite agree, Joseph. But this heat has made me thirsty," Rose said. "Excuse me for a moment. I think I'll go down and grab a glass of water." She turned to Jessie, one of the spinners. "You have enough water for you all, do you, Mrs Hunter?"

The old lady nodded, and bent her head again to her spinning.

Rose looked around at her busy new workroom, taking in the large windows that took up most of the walls. There had been two more visits from the Naval Inspector, and he had taken all the cloth they had. Jack Hayward had also made contact with Samuel Sparks of Viney Bridge Mill and other local mills, and approved the quality of their cloth.

Russell's Carriers were busier than ever, and the warehouse at Bridport was overflowing with merchandise.

A boat called the 'Mary Ellen,' named after Tom's mother, had been loaned from Jim Gilbert, and several deliveries of canvas had been made to Portsmouth. Life was going well for Rose, except for her underlying anxiety for Tom's welfare. Sea battles could be bloody, mutilating and at the worst, deadly. She shuddered. Would she ever see him again, or would he be slipped overboard wrapped in his own hammock to clear his dead body from the deck? Either way, it was something she couldn't bear to think about.

Chapter 16

Tom went back down through the hatch, and started to collect his belongings. There wasn't much; a spare monkey jacket and striped shirt, a picture of his family. His tin pot. Wasn't much to show for his life on board the ship.

His shipmates were still in discussion, saying their goodbyes and exchanging addresses. There were tears of course. Many friendships would be forged for life; others forgotten with the passing of the years.

"It's time we went," he said, turning away to pick up his bag to avoid revealing his raw emotion. For a moment he lingered, unready to leave the only home he had known for the past few months. The journey back from Gib had been terrible, with storms and strong winds, and he had been seasick most days. He should have been happy to go, but somehow it was as if he had a bond with these men; they had been through so much together.

Victory had anchored at the Solent, held back from entering Portsmouth by the tide, and now Tom joined his fellow seamen in the barge as they prepared to row towards the quay at Portsmouth. He looked around at the mates he had known for only a short time, and it filled him with pride knowing that, together with his shipmates, and sailmakers everywhere, he had enabled Nelson's fleet to defeat Napoleon.

He looked up at the mighty triple-decker that towered above the small boat, and in the darkness he tried to imagine the damage that had been done to the hull. The Victory had taken massive punishment from the French and Spanish guns, but he had been told that she was seaworthy enough to take Nelson, lying in his brandy soaked cask, and lashed to the deck, onto his final journey to London and a hero's funeral.

It had been strange to leave the sinister emptiness of the motionless ship and to emerge into the pervasive gloom. Seagulls mewed as they drifted about the ship, and now and again bells clanged and chains clanked, but otherwise the uneasy silence unnerved him. His tongue flicked over his dry lips and he swallowed hard, trying to rid himself of the lump in his throat. He hadn't realised that leaving the only home he had known for several months would be so difficult.

Without warning a sudden wind snatched his breath away, and as he gasped in the salty sea air he realised the enormity of all they had achieved. When he reached land no one would be waiting for him; he would have to find his own way home. Beyond the huddled red roofs of Portsmouth he knew that beyond them lay his real home and the welcome of his own loved ones.

After a while he became aware of the crowds in the distance; it was as if millions of people were waiting on the harbour for the Victory to dock and to welcome Britain's heroes home, but he imagined their disappointment when they realised there was no ship and no beloved Admiral.

As the barge reached the quayside, the cheering crowd became hushed as the word spread that Nelson was not amongst the landing crew. Little boats kept arriving and discharging their passengers, and the sailors were given room to disembark; even the doxies, bellies full of drink, lowered their eyes in respect as the sailors passed. Amongst the congratulations and thanks there was a general air of sadness and loss as people came forward to shake their hands and wish them well. There would be even more tomorrow.

Tom's ear had stopped throbbing, but he had become aware of open stares from children and veiled glances from their parents, always conscious of the congealed blood surrounding his disfigurement; he had kept it covered with his hand until told to remove it by Lieutenant Edward Williams.

"Never cover up your injuries lad," he advised. "Be proud of the way you have come by them, serving your King and country."

"Mind you," Tom confided to Jim later, "this isn't half as bad as some of the things I've witnessed. Have you seen old Joe's foot? He'll never get on a pair of boots again."

"There'll be a lot of limbs floating about the Mediterranean then," Jim replied with a grimace. "Wouldn't want to be picking one of them up at the shoreline."

A group of elderly ladies approached Tom, and thrust forward their spokeswoman.

Maggie took his hand and squeezed it enthusiastically. "I think you're ever so brave to fight them furriners, sir. We all think you sailormen so gallant. Ain't that right, girls?" Five heads nodded in unison. "Please, sir," she continued. "We was wondering...what 'ave you done with Lord Nelson? We thought he'd be with you."

Tom swallowed. What could he say? I'm sorry, he's dead, ladies? He'd hardly come to terms with it himself, and it was now up to him to relay the worst news of the century. As he struggled to find the words, Jim came up behind him and clapped him on the shoulder.

"Couldn't leave you alone five minutes before you're chatting up the ladies." He winked at Maggie. "'Though I wouldn't blame him. You're a real beauty, did you know that?"

The old lady blushed, and a dimple appeared amongst her wrinkles. "I was asking this young man what you've done with Lord Nelson."

Now it was Jim's turn to feel uncomfortable. "I'm afraid he died, my love," he said gently.

"Oh, no!" Her face crumpled, and she sank to her knees.

"I thought that man were wonderful," she said breathlessly. "Whatever are we going to do without him? Oh, Gladys. I don't think I can bear it."

"Hush, Maggie dear." Gladys took her fan from her bag and handed it to her. She sat down with her on the quayside and tenderly held her friend until she composed herself.

"Where are all the ships, and what have they done with Nelson's body, then?" Maggie asked, a frown creasing her forehead. "We would so like to see it."

"Oh, he won't be brought off here," Tom said. "I believe there are other plans."

"'Tis typical of them scheming politishuns," Gladys said crossly. "We'd give 'im a splendid send off. We would, you know," she said, putting her hands on her hips, glaring at the gathering crowd as if to seek verification.

"I know you would, Gladys," Tom said gently. "But as he was a very important man he'll have a special funeral, I expect. In London."

"Well, I don't know," the old lady muttered. "We'm never good enough for things like that. 'Tis all they Londoners what's going to benefit from all them shenanigans."

Tom and Jim were surrounded by an excited mob all wanting information, and when two men tried to enter the group the coarser of the two kicked Tom, and the other grabbed Jim's arm.

"You. What's being done with Admiral Nelson's body?" Tom's attacker asked roughly.

"Where are all them boats? How did you get here? What 'aven't we been told? Are the French coming ter get us?" His friend cracked his knuckles threateningly.

"Calm down," bellowed Tom in desperation. "You're safe." He wanted to shout the good news from the rooftops, but he merely repeated his statement. "Nelson's body is on board the Victory on the Solent," he explained, "but she is held back by the tide. She'll dock tomorrow morning, if you wish to see her then. Nelson's body will then be taken to London," he added. "Most of the enemy were sunk, many of the French and Spanish sailors died, and no-one's coming to get us. All right? It was a total victory. So, if you don't mind, everyone. I'll be on my way. I have a home to get to."

Gradually the mob dispersed, and the men from the Victory walked through the crowd, recognised by their blue and red jackets, and their strange way of walking with a swaying motion as they adjusted to solid ground. The word had spread, and now voices became hushed, a muffled sound of moaning turning to weeping as people discovered their loss; hands reached out to touch and to shake the hands with the crew, for now, questions frozen on frightened lips.

Tom needed to get away from the outpouring of grief. Would it always be like this, he wondered? He knew that he would be made to relive it over and over again until he was sick of it. And then he would remind himself that he was one of the lucky ones, that he should share his first-hand knowledge with those who would have wanted to be there, to have met the great Nelson, to be told of his last hours.

He pushed his tarpaulin hat firmly down over his long pigtail and went in search of the George Inn. His shipmates had broken free of the crowd, and had spread out to wander through the narrow streets of Portsmouth looking for coaches to hire, getting lifts in any vehicle they could find.

Jim followed discreetly, his excuse being that Tom needed time on his own, and stopped to talk to several full-breasted doxies swaying drunkenly outside an inn.

Tom stopped so that he could catch up. "Wasn't that one of your women back there?" He winked.

Jim sighed. "Them days have gone," he said wistfully. "I've got me wife waiting for me at home."

"Mr Tom Welland?"

"Who wants to know?"

A plain, pimply youth standing on the corner by the George Inn, held out a letter, and as soon as Tom took it he scarpered.

The expression on Tom's face changed instantly from one of affability to one of bafflement. "Now who would be writing to me at Portsmouth?" he said as he ripped open the envelope and read the contents. "Oh. That's nice. That's very nice." His voice rose in surprise. "God bless you, Squire Seymour."

Jim hovered impatiently. "Well?"

"My village has made a collection for a stagecoach so that I can ride home in style. What d'you make of that?"

"Would that be travelling on the inside or the outside?"

"I don't have to pay, so I shall sit in comfort. Sitting outside for several days in December will no doubt give me frostbite or something worse."

"I live in Somerset, too," Jim said hopefully. "In Crewkerne."

Tom laughed. "You and I have been at sea together for months and we didn't know we lived near each other. Wait a minute."

Tom disappeared into the George and Jim waited until he came back.

"It gets better," Tom grinned. "Father's asked me to find William Browne. Apparently he was on the Achilles, and I feel that I should know him, but I can't place him. Landlord says the stagecoach will be waiting in the yard. Be ready in ten minutes."

"But what about Will Browne?"

"Don't worry about him. He'll turn up. He knows where to come. Oh, and by the way. There's a change of clothing in my room. Seems that's been donated by Squire Seymour too."

"But I thought…"

"I can't stand the man, but I should imagine he's crowing about us now. Knowing two Victory men from the village will be quickest way he'll ever get to Parliament."

Suddenly Jim grabbed him and pushed him through the doorway of the inn. "For God's sake, hide somewhere," he said urgently. "Those two ruffians must have stirred up the crowd, and a mob is coming down the street after us."

Tom charged recklessly through the parlour, with Jim close behind, on his way to find the landlord, accidentally tripping up an elderly gentleman with a pint of grog in his hand as he made his way to his table.

"I'm so sorry," muttered Tom, as he stopped to clean up the mess, but Jim caught the neck of his jacket and hauled him away.

"Go out the back!" he ordered.

A tall, thin man, whom Tom took to be the landlord, suddenly appeared barred their way. "We don't want no troublemakers in 'ere," he snapped. "Get out of my inn and don't come back."

"But you don't understand," gasped Tom. "There's a gang out there…"

But he advanced no further. Somebody grabbed him from behind and pushed him towards the door, and he was at the point of being thrown out when a party of revellers forced their way in, spreading out around the tables and the bar, blocking the doorways and sealing off the room, making escape impossible.

"We want to speak to them sailors over there, and especially the one what's 'ad 'is ear eaten by an 'orse."

The lad's voice was high pitched, and he appeared to be cross-eyed. A globule of spittle had formed at the corner of his slack mouth, and he showered his companions as he spoke.

"Take no notice of 'im," snarled a handsome youth, who clicked his fingers to the barmaid, and instantly a drink appeared on a nearby table. "We want to know if they're who they say they are. We've been told they were on the Victory, Nelson's ship. Seems there was a battle, and Nelson was killed. Well, we ain't heard of no Nelson, or his Victory, but if there is, we want to know about it."

Bravely the landlord confronted them.

"If these men are from the Victory they'll be tired, and need their beds," he said sternly. "They are nothing to do with you, but you are frightening my customers and interrupting their meals. Get out. Get out, all of you, and I would advise you all to go home before you're arrested."

"Actually no, it's not all right." The ringleader wiped his nose with the back of his hand. "Me and the others. We're going to stay right here until we talk to them. There's money to be made out of this."

"Come on Jake. Leave them alone. There's plenty of other sailors about." A pretty girl, about twenty years old, caught his hand and tried to drag him away, but he shrugged her off.

"We want to speak to them now," demanded the bully, pulling out a knife and holding it to a barmaid's cheek. A woman screamed, and for a moment the room was full of people, overturned chairs and tables as everyone made for the door.

"Quick. There's a door behind the bar. You can use the room first on the left at the top of the stairs," hissed the landlord, handing Tom a key. "Go out the back door when you've finished."

Up in the bedroom Tom borrowed some clothes that had been left in the closet and changed into them, handing Jim a cloak that he found in the dresser. "I'll send him my name and address," Tom said, as he pulled on his boots and made for a side entrance.

The coach was splendid. Its newly painted blue and gold exterior sported the name 'Lord Nelson' on the side, and Tom was surprised to see that the coachman was dressed fashionably, wearing a cloth box coat, and a neat cravat. He raised his white beaver hat in the form of a greeting.

"Hurry up, we need to get going," hissed Jim, and jumped into the stagecoach. But once inside, he became aware of a figure concealed in a cloak sitting by the window.

"Who the hell are you?" he demanded.

The stranger's voice was muffled, but the accent was revealing.

"Will Browne! Nice to meet you." Jim held out his hand.

"I thought there were three of us." Will lowered the hood of his cloak.

"There should be." Jim said, as he opened the window and leaned out.

"Tom. I've found Will. What the hell are you doing? Hurry up. That mob will be here in a minute. Come on!"

The guard removed the horse cloths and jumped up behind the coachman. As Tom boarded the coach it started to move. Suddenly one of the gang appeared, then another and another, until they had surrounded the coach.

"Let's get 'em."

With a lad at each of the doors trying to pull them open, several on the roof, and another trying to frighten the horses, the guard blew his horn, the coachman signalled to the ostler that he was ready to go, and with a slight yielding of his rein hand, the coach was off. The lads fell back, rolling clear of the wheels of the stagecoach as it headed for the archway, and soon it was rumbling through the narrow streets of Portsmouth with its precious cargo. The lads were on their way home.

Chapter 17

The men settled back in their seats and tried to make themselves comfortable. Tom picked up a bundle of papers and rifled through them, then handed a map book to Will.

"Have a look. See where we're going. I was asking the coachman which inn he was heading for, and he said we should take a short break at a country inn before going on to Southampton. We can have a shave and get some breakfast there."

"Wherever we go we're going to get mobbed," Jim said gloomily.

"That's why I hid in here." Will said. "It can't be avoided. People are bound to get very excited when a national hero is killed in the course of his duty, especially when he has won a great victory. The best we can do is to accept it gracefully, but at the same time we must take care that none of us is hurt, which is why it has been arranged that we shall be protected by the management at each inn that we visit. I have received a letter from Squire Seymour explaining that we shall be made as comfortable as possible, and that we can take advantage of all the facilities, as everything has been paid for."

Tom felt sorry for Will. He was tall, almost tall enough for his head to poke through the roof so that he could say 'hello' to the driver. His legs were bent awkwardly to fit into the small space between the seats, and his arms forced into an uncomfortable position as he tried to make the best use of the dying light to read the map book.

Will tapped a page of the book with his finger. "The Rose at Holborn Bridge. That's the one. A private room has been hired so that we can answer any questions the public put to us, but I have been reminded that the dispatches have not yet arrived, and the official version of events has not yet been revealed, so we must be careful what we say. I'm not sure yet whether the King has been informed."

Tom wondered when William Browne would smile. He seemed pompous, smug even, but he had the feeling that there was more to this man than he first thought. His eyes were dark and unfathomable, yet the corners of his mouth were upturned, as he were used to smiling, given the right incentive. He thought it strange that he had never met him before, but then Jim lived in the next village and he had never heard of him.

Tom closed his eyes and settled back into his seat, trying to sleep. But the road was uneven and bumpy, and despite the newness of the carriage springs they were jostled about over the stones of Portsmouth. He had bitten his tongue, and now he longed for the taste of real ale to rid himself of the taste of blood.

At last his mind centred on home, and upon his family. What would he find on his return? He pulled his cloak more tightly round him to keep out the draught, and with his eyes half closed allowed his mind wander. He found himself humming one of the tunes he had sung to Ben as a baby, after his wife had died, and the child wouldn't settle. Twinkle, twinkle, little star, a carol for Christmas. Ben had lain completely still, his eyes open, staring at him, and at that moment it seemed as if the baby, their baby, felt her loss as deeply as himself. Rebecca had been his one love, his kindred spirit, and her death had made him feel as if he had been torn in half. He hadn't been able to survive as an incomplete person and his world started to fall apart until his parents intervened, and took both son and grandchild under their wing. They had been his salvation.

Then Rose had come along. Rose and her daughter Emily, and he had fallen in love all over again. Then after his father died and his mother had gone away for a while, Rose and he had grown closer and their children had played together as brother and sister. Their dream of creating a new business was becoming reality, and then at the worst possible moment he had had to leave her to go to battle. How was she managing in his absence, he wondered, without knowing whether he was alive or dead? His lips curved into a smile as he imagined her reaction when she realised he had survived.

He was brought back to reality by rustling paper as Jim turned to a fresh page of the Times.

"This copy's too old," he grumbled. "I don't want to know yesterday's news. I want to know how much people have been told. It's too dark to read anyway," he said, as he tidied the newspaper away into his bag. He sighed. "All I want is to get home, have a good wash, lots of food and beer and a long sleep. And make love to me missus. Is that too much to ask?"

"This mobbing business is really getting to you, isn't it?" Tom grinned. "Afraid your good looks will attract too many women? I'm sure you can cope, old feller."

Self-consciously Tom reached up and touched his damaged ear. Would it affect Rose's feelings towards him, he wondered, or would she be relieved that it had been his only injury? Would she be proud when he told her that he had been at the centre of a battle that altered the course of history? He smiled. Perhaps it would make her fancy him even more! But what would he think when he looked into a mirror? Would his disfigurement be worse than he imagined? But then, for the hundredth time he would remind himself that he had been one of the lucky ones.

His thoughts were interrupted by Will, who accidentally nudged him as he put his hand into his pocket to bring out some pieces of bread. He handed them around.

"Have either of you ever been into the dockyard?" he asked. "I mean, really into the dockyard at Portsmouth?"

"Can't say I really thought about it. I was too busy trying to get myself home," Tom said thoughtfully.

"The smell of fresh bread was too appealing for a starving man, so I hoped that someone would take pity on me and feed me." Will smiled ruefully. "Of course, I couldn't resist looking around. I saw the sail loft, the rigging house, almost as high as it was long. You should have seen it, Tom, it was amazing. Didn't think I'd get the chance again. The retting pond must have been at least four hundred feet long, with sea water flowing into it through big sluices, with dozens of masts and yards floating in it."

"I didn't think you'd be interested in that sort of thing, Will," put in Jim. "Just what sort of trade were you in before the battle?"

"I fattened the odd cow now and then. In fact, I've been thinking lately of growing flax. Would it be more profitable, d'you think?"

"Don't know much about beef," replied Tom. "But if you really want to consider a change of job maybe we can talk. Depends on lots of things." Determined not to dwell on his relationship between sailmaking and its contribution to the English fleet, Tom filled his mouth with another chunk of bread and chewed. "That tastes good," he said. "Got any more?"

"Didn't have room in me pocket." Will brushed the crumbs from his breeches, and when he looked up again, Tom thought he could see the light of determination in his eyes.

"D'you know, I never realised ship's cables were so huge; s'pose they have to be, really, considering the size of ships nowadays. No-one was there, so I went into the rigging house and had a look around. Upstairs they make the twine and prepare the yarn, while downstairs the threads are twisted together. Is that what a ropework does?"

"Sort of, but in a much smaller way. I'll tell you about it sometime."

"But I..."

"One day, perhaps," Tom said shortly. "I don't want to think about making sails for a while. I need a rest."

Tom was in a possessive mood. For one thing, he wasn't too happy about Will's fascination with his business, and for another, he wasn't sure if he liked him. He didn't want him meddling in something he didn't understand.

"Weren't you listening to me?" Will said angrily. "You seem determined to ignore me. We are all tired, but that doesn't stop me showing an interest in your business. I wish you no harm, Tom, but please do me the courtesy of listening to what I am saying."

Tom sighed. "I'm sorry, Will. I was listening, really I was. I didn't want to bore you with my life, but if you're serious, and looking for work, I might be able to help. No promises, mind."

Will 's outburst was soon over. "That would be good. Thanks, I'd appreciate that," he said, settling back into the seat and closing his eyes.

But Tom was uneasy. An employee with a short temper was not a good idea, and he decided that should Will approach him with a request for work he would find a believable excuse to turn him down.

A short while later the three men were disturbed from sleep when the guard blew his horn as a warning that they were about to change horses. The coachman and guard dismounted, coming around to the side of the coach to open the doors.

The driver removed his hat before speaking. "Perhaps you would like to take a drink at this inn before we continue, gentlemen. We don't have long, and I think for your own sakes it would be a good idea if we were to continue the journey as soon as possible. About ten minutes?"

"What a wonderfully upper class accent he has," Tom commented. "I suppose it comes with the cut of his cloth. And what manners! I wonder where he comes from?"

The landlord, a man in his forties, came to the door of the inn, and, moving with an ape-like gait, led the way down a long narrow passage. "I have reserved a private room for you, gentlemen," he said, ushering them into a beautifully decorated, typically Georgian dining room, with a thick carpet and upholstered chairs in blue and gold.

"If you would care to help yourselves from the range of drinks set out on the table, gentlemen, you will be most welcome, and as you are short of time, I have arranged for a package of food to be given to you to last until your next stopping place. These offerings are supplied free by the management in recognition of your services to our country, and for which we are humbly grateful."

"Wasn't that generous?" Tom said, as they climbed back into their carriage.

The guard and driver remounted; a quick blow on the horn, a sleight easing of the reins, and they were off again.

"No sign of any sightseers," Jim sounded disappointed.

"If you want to be mobbed and clubbed over the head then stay." Will yawned. "To be honest, Jim, I can't wait to get my head down for a few hours." He tried to stretch his legs to get into a more comfortable position for sleep, but succeeded only in kicking Jim in the knee. The older man flinched.

"Hey. Look what you're doing, you clumsy oaf." Jim pushed Will's legs away from him before rolling up his cloak and putting it under his head. "Wake me up when we arrive at Southampton," he said, closing his eyes.

The road was smoother now, and after a while Tom slept, and for several hours the three men took a well-earned rest.

Suddenly two horse-riders came alongside, and sensing trouble the driver cracked his whip, urging his team of horses into a canter. The coach started to rock violently as the wheels ran over rough ground, and Tom was jolted awake. Concerned at the accelerating speed, he lurched towards the window, tripping over his sleeping companions as he pulled up the sash. As he leaned out the riders came alongside, and he pulled the window down with a bang.

"Will that damn gang of idiots ever give up" he exclaimed angrily, waking his travelling companions as he stumbled around the carriage trying to find his seat. "We didn't go through that battle just to get killed on the highroad. Isn't there something we can do?"

The horses' hooves clanged over the macadamised road, their harnesses rattling as the animals sped on at a smart gallop, going faster and faster to shake off their pursuers, the passengers bouncing around inside the coach like a set of nine pins. Eventually houses began to appear at either side of the road, and the riders dropped back as they approached the paved streets of Southampton.

The guard sounded his horn, and the carriage slowed, the horses all sweat and foam as they pulled into the yard of the Rose Inn. The coachman threw down the reins and dismounted, running around to the carriage door and opening it for his disoriented passengers to alight.

"I'm bloody cold, I feel as if I've lost me sea legs and turned into a jelly fish," moaned Jim. "Me insides are as sore as me bottom and I can't stand up."

"Stop whinging," said Tom. "At least we're here and in one piece, aren't we? What's a few bruises? I'm looking forward to a wash, some supper and a good night's sleep. What about you, Will?"

"I think we should get inside, just in case any of those madmen have managed to follow us. Let's hope they didn't see us come in here."

The only other people in the yard were two stable lads who had come to look after the horses, whilst the landlord, a man in his forties, appeared in the doorway flapping his hands in agitation.

"I was expecting you," he said abruptly. "Come with me, gentlemen," he said, steering his guests like a flock of sheep along a paved and covered passageway towards the reception hall. From there they were taken to a small side room, where he spoke to them in confidence.

"I am afraid we have rather a problem, gentlemen," he said in a low voice. "It would seem that a considerable number of the public are trying to find their way in, and it is proving difficult to keep them out. They say they will not leave until you speak to them. What would you like me to do?"

"Damn. I spoke too soon," Tom said, running a hand impatiently through his thick brown hair. "We've had a lot of bother with a gang of men ever since we left Portsmouth," he explained. "I was hoping we'd lost them, but they are very persistent. They seem determined to hound us until we give them what we want."

"What do they want?" The landlord seemed baffled.

"They want a full account of the battle, at the very least," Jim said uncomfortably. "I'm afraid it could get out of hand if we don't give in. Do you think we should speak to them?" he asked, looking at Tom.

"No. Definitely not, Tom said. "I want to keep our whereabouts secret for the time being. For obvious reasons the news will spread all over the country before an official letter is written, or a despatch sent, so they can wait.

Landlord. I would like you please to issue strict instructions to your staff that they are not to accept bribes for information. Could you do that, please?"

"Of course," the landlord said briskly. He clapped his hands. "I need to see all my members of staff immediately," he called.

But when they did not appear the balding, portly man visibly seemed to melt; a tic formed in one eye and his breathing deteriorated.

"I'm sorry gentlemen," he said, mopping his forehead with a large handkerchief. "I can assure you they will be here soon. Wait a minute while I go and check."

"I think you should sit down and rest," Tom said firmly. "I don't think you're well."

"No, no. That simply will not do. I insist…"

"Don't worry. We can handle it, can't we gentlemen?"

Will and Jim nodded.

There was a crash and the sound of tinkling glass.

"But they are breaking in…my public house…" The landlord started to run from the room, but Tom stopped him at the doorway.

"Don't worry. We'll deal with it. Calm down, sir." Tom took the man's elbow and steered him towards a chair, and weakly the landlord sat down.

"Sit there, please sir," Tom said respectfully, but to Will he whispered, "Make him stay in it. I'm going to see what's happened. And to Jim, "If they happen to come in there's nothing you can do on your own and," he added, jerking his head towards the landlord, "he's in a pretty bad way. They may beat the doors down and smash their way through this place until there's nothing left, but I don't want anyone hurt. They won't go away until they're satisfied, but we can't tell them anything. Not yet, anyway. They're only interested in the money they can make out of us. And whatever you do don't follow me, it's too dangerous."

The noise grew louder as he walked down the corridor; from here it seemed as if the whole of Portsmouth was outside the Rose Inn, and when Tom entered the coffee room the staff were in the process of barricading the outer doors by piling tables and chairs against them. By now several members of the mob had entered the room through a broken window and were setting about the staff with shards of glass.

Tom jumped onto a table and took a pistol from his pocket. He had put it there before he left the Victory, more as a souvenir from the battle than from any intention of using it, and throughout the long journey home the weight of it had felt reassuring.

The pistol was still loaded, and now he pressed the trigger, firing several shots into the ceiling.

It had the desired effect, and for a moment everything was quiet… but then the fighting started. More and more people arrived and joined in, fists and feet flying as they piled on top of each other, and for the moment, Tom was ignored.

The mob was out for a good time, and violence seemed to be part of it. They were full of drink, and wanted more; employees were tied up and pushed outside into the cold night as the mob set about ransacking the cellar for barrels of ale.

They were wearing ribbons in their hats and laurel around their necks, which Tom suspected had been ripped from the bushes outside the inn, and as the drink began to flow the revellers became merry. They were ripe for a celebration, yet in their drunken state they had forgotten that the three sought after sailors were right under their noses. They had heard that a battle had been won and their country freed from Napoleon's tyranny, yet they were ignoring the one person who could tell them all they needed to know.

Suddenly Jake swaggered into the room with an armful of sticks, and threw them to his friends. Four of them leaped onto the bar and started to sweep aside empty glasses and bottles, whilst several others followed his lead, smashing the rest of the windows and furniture.

Tom leapt down from the table and ran for the door, opened it and ran down the passage. It wouldn't be long before Jake realised he had gone, and would come after him.

But it was not to be. As he crept along the passage to the outer door he met Jim and Will coming the other way, followed by their captors.

Tom sauntered past them, feigning ignorance, and when he reached the next doorway along he dived into it, closing the door quietly behind him.

But not for long. The rioters had recognised him, and forced their way in to the room. After they had taken his pistol away from him Tom was dragged along the corridor and escorted back to the coffee room, where Jim and Will were waiting for him.

They were surrounded and questions fired at them.

"What was Nelson like? Were you there when he was killed? What did you do? And what stuff did you steal off the ship?"

The Navy men remained silent.

"I'm asking you one more time," Jake threatened. "Whatever trinkets you stole from the ship I want you to hand them over. Now."

When Tom finally spoke, his voice was controlled, but full of sadness. "We didn't steal from Nelson's ship. There was very little left after the battle, unless you count dead bodies, bits of limbs, and headless torsos. Everything over the side."

"I don't believe you," Jake said angrily. "If you don't give them to us we'll kill you and take them anyway."

Tom laughed. "After what we've been through I'm not giving you anything, except for a bit of advice. Think how stupid you'll look, killing men who have just come through a terrifying battle. Real heroes, the lot of you!"

Jake ignored him.

"I want you to tell us how you won the battle," he demanded. You must have some interesting stories to tell."

"And let you sell them to the newspapers? Oh no. We couldn't do that."

"Grab 'em," cried the ringleader. "We'll make 'em talk. And don't worry. We'll be making money out of you." He turned and spoke to his friends. "Gentlemen," he said, "there's a fortune to be made here"

The three men were seized and their pockets rifled, and Jake, realising that Tom had told the truth, grabbed a handful of his hair, jerked his head backwards and produced his knife, holding it to his throat.

"You must have something. Where is it?"

Tom saw the determination in Jake's eyes as he felt the tip of the knife slicing through his skin, and the trickle of blood running down his chest, but he said nothing. This was bad, but nothing could be as bad as Trafalgar!

"Speak!"

The knife cut deeper.

"Not interested." Tom shrugged. "If anyone is to tell the papers it will be me. And I don't think you'd have much sympathy if you were to be painted as a load of murderous villains more interested in filling their pockets than helping three tired sailors who have recently taken part in a battle and are desperately in need of their beds. Do you?"

"Who would know if we killed you?" Jake smirked. "And anyway, you don't have nothing worth robbing. Although it won't be as satisfying, we'll beat you up instead."

"Yeah. Beat 'em up, beat 'em up," chanted the mob. "That'll make 'em talk."

Will was struggling with his captors, and as he staggered to his feet, he spat at them. "You are beyond contempt," he raged. "How would any of you like to face a broadside from an enemy ship, showered with round shot, and blasted with noise whilst the rotten stench of powder smoke blinds and chokes you? Or perhaps you'd rather lie on a hard table with a gag in your mouth waiting in agony for the surgeon's knife to cut your leg off with a metal saw? You wouldn't be so brave then."

Jake paled, but kept the knife levelled at Tom's throat. Two of the women fainted and had to be carried away. Jim had been badly winded by a punch to his stomach, and was rolling in agony around the floor.

Tom's anger had been slow burning, but now he'd had enough. He was tired, and he wanted to get home. These stupid people had no morals; they had no consciences either. They were unable to understand the difference between right and wrong, and rather than feeling outrage he felt pity. What did they have in this world if they saw money as the central purpose for their existence, rather than pride in their country, and for a man like Nelson who had died for their freedom? And how dare they hurt Jim, who had been one of the bravest men he had ever known, refusing to lie down when the air was thick with musket balls. He felt responsible for him, offering him a lift when he could have been safely on his way by now.

"I still think 'e were bitten by an 'oss, whatever he says," sniggered Joe Bowden, the words slurred as his misshapen lips tried to form words his tongue was unable to form. "'e be lying, Jake. 'e never were on that ship. I think we should kill 'em all, now." The man giggled stupidly, and there was an embarrassed silence.

It was now or never. Tom looked purposefully at the door, then at Will, and back again to the door.

Will gave an imperceptible nod, Jim's head turned slightly as he followed the signal, and as Tom's arm jerked suddenly upwards, the knife fell to the floor, and the three men ran for their lives.

Chapter 18

"Do you gentlemen need help?" The speaker was dressed in the uniform of the local militia, and had appeared, as if by magic, in the passageway.

"Yes, Yes, We would. Thank you." His eyes darted nervously about the passage, and he glanced behind him, hoping they had not been seen.

The militiaman took pity on them. He had heard the alarm in the sailor's voice, and his friends seemed frightened and apprehensive.

"Quick. Come in here," he said, and stood back to allow the two sailors to enter a side room.

Several soldiers were sitting in groups talking, and looked up when they entered.

"We need your help," Tom said abruptly. "A mob of revellers followed us from Portsmouth when we docked and they've wrecked the coffee room. And stabbed our friend."

"We've only just arrived…" The militiaman looked at his comrades.

"Wait here." Boots were pulled on, rifles loaded, and the men filed through the door. Minutes later Tom heard the sound of running feet, a female voice raised in anger and then a piercing scream. Pistol shots followed, and then the clattering of hooves as a coach was driven out of the yard and up the road at full gallop.

The door opened and Jim entered the room. A crust of dried blood showed at the corner of his eye, but otherwise he seemed fine.

"Lads, I'm ready for my supper." Jim grinned. "You should see the bedroom. Better than a tart's boudoir! Oh, and by the way. I've thanked everyone for their help, and to make amends for their fright I've agreed that we'll talk to the staff in the morning, after we've seen the barber." He stroked his stubble. "Barmaids aren't too bad, either."

Suddenly he swayed and tried to steady himself, and Tom moved swiftly to catch him before he fell.

"Never mind the bloody barmaids," Tom said." Are you all right?"

"Leave me alone, Tom." Jim gasped as he staggered into the dining room before collapsing into a chair. He was breathing heavily and sweating profusely.

"Where did they stab you?" Tom opened his jacket, loosened the neck of his shirt and with his fingers gently probed an area of bloody tissue close to his shoulder.

"You were lucky, my friend," Tom said, as he accepted a piece of torn tablecloth from Will to pad the wound.

"It's not that bad." Jim protested weakly.

"It could be. Sit quietly for a while, and sip this."

Tom offered him a glass of water and he gulped it greedily.

"Have they gone?" Jim tried to turn his head, and he winced.

"Militia's seen them villains off. They stole a carriage but they'll soon be picked up. I reckon they won't be coming back in a hurry." Will said. He rubbed his hands together. "Now, what are we having?" He picked up the menu but after a few moments he laid it back down on the table.

"I forgot. I can't read." He handed the menu to Tom. "What d'you recommend, old friend?"

Tom snatched the paper, crumpled it and threw it onto the table. "How insensitive can you be, Will? If you want to eat go somewhere else. I can't bear to be in the same room as you."

"Well, I'm hungry. We've still got some way to go, and we deserve a little spoiling."

With envy Will surveyed a group of customers sitting at a nearby table tucking into a large chicken.

"Well, if I can't eat I might order a drop of their best port."

"Please yourself," Tom said. "I'm taking Jim to his bed. He needs medical attention, and one way or another I'll see that he gets it."

Tom tried to sleep, but his joints were stiff and painful, and lying in a motionless bed seemed strange. He had become used to the gentle swinging of his hammock whilst at sea; he had learned to sleep through any amount of noise, but now his slumber was continually disturbed by the unfamiliar clatter of coaches and guard horns in the road outside. He awoke feeling tired and drained of energy, nearly falling asleep over his breakfast of ham and eggs.

Jim's wound had been taken care of, and now he was sitting opposite Tom and Will, filling his face with food. His spirits had risen at the thought of being so close to home, and he had even joked that he was looking forward to seeing his wife.

The road to Salisbury was heavy with traffic. Wagons, drays and vehicles of all descriptions struggled through incessant rain and a biting easterly wind that hampered the horses. Inside their coach the men shivered, despite pulling their cloaks around their legs and their shawls over their noses.

The countryside itself was desolate and monotonous; those sailors with occasional transport had managed with very little sleep since leaving their ships, and now joined the soldiers trudging home to the West Country, their uniforms splattered with mud from the wheels of vehicles, bound for their destinations on the south-west coast.

The travellers slept fitfully for a while, but after a twenty-minute break and a change of horses they were away again, refreshed and prepared for the rest of the journey.

The weather was cold but dry, although black clouds threatened in the distance. The coachman urged his horses into a gallop, so that both he and his passengers would reach the comfort of an inn before rain set in.

Tom passed around boxes of food prepared for them at their last stop, and once they'd eaten, Will broke the silence.

"I don't suppose you want to discuss our little skirmish, do you lads?" he asked hopefully. "I haven't liked to bring up the subject before now because I didn't know how either of you felt about it. I suppose it's a period of our lives that will never be forgotten, and although I would never want to go through it all again, the memories will remain vivid for the rest of my life."

Tom's anger had not yet subsided, but he could see no point in prolonging the feeling of resentment. And besides, he was intrigued to learn more about the battle from someone else's point of view.

Jim had turned his head towards the window, seemingly mesmerised by the wind gusting through the poplars by the side of the road, no doubt absorbed in thoughts of his own.

"You were with Captain King of the Achilles, weren't you?" Tom scratched his head. "I seem to remember your ship led the lee line whilst we took the windward. I saw the French ships forming a crescent shape before we went to breakfast, and then suddenly we were in the middle of it. Victory fired the first broadside into Villeneuve's Bucentaure, raking her decks. Did a lot of damage. Enough to wreck her, I'm told. After that we ran aboard the Redoubtable and broke the line. She retaliated fiercely and her fire brought down our foretopsail and shot away her wheel. Several men were killed. What happened to you?"

"We followed the Collossus into action, chasing after the Spanish Montanez until she sheered off. Pretty soon we set off to help our Belleisle, which had been dismasted, but got caught by the Spanish Argonauta. Captain King came onto her port beam and set about her for at least an hour. She pretended to surrender, but before we could take her the French Achille passed us and started firing at us. Then that damn French Berwick put herself between us and the Argonauta, who took off, and we found ourselves pitching in to the Berwick, but we dealt with her, all right. We lost heavily, thirteen killed and fifty nine wounded. Her masts and bowsprit and hull were wrecked but we slaughtered a lot of Berwick's crew with our broadsides. Other than that, quite a successful day, wasn't it?"

"How can you say that?" said Tom angrily. "Maybe we beat the Combined Fleet, but at what a price! Four hours of battle, thousands dead. Nelson gone. How can you say the day was a success?" He paused, and the darkness of despair settled over him as he remembered. The scene of devastation was indelibly printed on his mind, and now he started to speak slowly but distinctly as he relieved the horror of that day.

"The sun had gone down, and the Combined Fleet were badly mauled and helpless. Seventeen French and Spanish fleets had been captured and the eighteenth blown up. We had done well, not one of our twenty-seven ships had been sunk or forced to strike. The swell of the sea and the high clouds had merged into an ominous grey sheet. Two days later a gale was blowing, the wind screamed and the sea was heaving. Fifteen ships had been destroyed, eight prizes taken, but only four made it to Gibraltar Apart from the French and Spanish, one Admiral was killed, another wounded. Two Captains killed; four Captains wounded. On the night of the battle, Hardy had done his best to secure the fore and main masts, and somehow had managed to wear the ship around.

The ship started to break up, and all hands manned the pumps, but the Victory was drifting helplessly in the middle of a strong gale.

At dawn we could see that the Royal Sovereign was flying a distress signal, and Hardy sent the Polyphemus to help her. In the afternoon, after the wind had dropped a bit, Thomas Freemantle from the Neptune took Victory in tow."

"Granted, it was a bloody terrible day," Will said, "but our Captain did us proud. He risked his life on many occasions to keep our ship safe."

Jim turned away from the window and settled back in his seat and belched loudly. "Ah, that's better," he said, and shifted his position on the seat. "I feel more comfortable now. Must have been that piece of onion. It never did agree with me. Were you talking about Thomas Hardy? I don't know whether you are aware that he comes from Crewkerne."

"Really?" Tom's raised his eyebrows. "I have a lot of time for that man. Isn't it amazing how many of us live close to each other?"

"Hardy went to Crewkerne Grammar School. " Jim chuckled." I remember my father telling me that every Shrove Tuesday the boys were allowed to indulge in cock fighting in the schoolroom. The cocks were armed with steel spurs, and after the fight the winner was expected to recite poetry. Can you imagine Hardy, that big hearty man, doing that?"

"That's to assume he won," Will said with a grin.

"I wonder if he knew the Hood family," Tom said thoughtfully.

"Never heard of them," Jim admitted. "Should I have?"

"Never heard of the Hoods?" Tom was scandalised. "Sam and Alex were just about the best seamen I have ever met, apart from Nelson. They're friendly with a neighbour of mine." He had a sudden thought. "I wonder if they knew Thomas Hardy when he lived at Crewkerne. Their father was the vicar of Thorncombe and a master at the Crewkerne Grammar School."

"Hardy always seemed to know what he was doing," said Jim, brightening a little. "Perhaps that's why he got on so well with Nelson. If Nelson was unhappy, Hardy cheered him up with that ringing laugh of his. I shall miss that."

"He was rarely wrong about anything," Tom said. "Nelson trusted him, and it was obvious they thought a lot of each other."

"I wonder where he is now?" Jim said thoughtfully. "I might look him up when I get home, unless he's on another of those naval engagements of his."

For a while they sat in companionable silence, each thinking their own thoughts, whilst outside thick fog swirled around the carriage, shrouding the countryside, intensifying the ringing of the horses hooves as they pounded the open road.

The three weary sailors were nearly home.

At the end of October Lapenotiere took a pouch containing Collingwood's dispatches and Blackwood's letters from his desk and climbed aboard the schooner 'Pickle.' The dispatch was to be sent to Lord Barham at the Admiralty in London, over two hundred and fifty miles away.

On November the third, after a bad journey, Pickle arrived at Falmouth, where Lieutenant Lapenotiere took a jolly boat to meet frigates waiting to carry the message to Plymouth. From there he travelled by post-chaise through Exeter and Axminster on his way to London, where he encountered thick banks of fog, showing yellow in the lamplight. His throat tightened with the abrasive taste of sulphur, which slowed him down, and he cursed in frustration.

At about one o'clock in the morning Lapenotiere's carriage turned through the arch into the Admiralty's cobbled courtyard, but the First Sea Lord had retired to bed. He was roused and spent some time perusing the dispatches, and at five o' clock a messenger was sent to inform His Majesty. And at eight o'clock the Prince of Wales, the Duke of York, Prime Minister Mr Pitt and the Lord Mayor were informed. Like the rest of the populace, a feeling of sorrow for the death of Nelson overshadowed the ending of the threat of invasion.

Rumours of Nelson's death spread throughout the city like wildfire. Illuminations dazzled thousands, guns boomed out, and as soon as newspapers were printed they were rushed out to readers in the capital and on the continent anxious to discover if Nelson really was dead.

Before long, shop windows had been draped with purple cloth, and people were wearing black crepe, going about their business silently, or with a murmur of respect and sorrow for their country's great loss.

But the travellers were unaware of this as they slept fitfully in their carriage as they were taken towards their final destination. The news had already reached most of the country, and the knowledge that their men folk were coming home had caused great excitement amongst family, friends and neighbours. Throughout West Country towns and villages parties were being prepared for the return of the heroes, bell ringers were practicing joyful refrains, and beer had already started to flow.

Mary had laid aside her spinning and the accounts to concentrate on making mementoes to welcome the boys home. Sailmaking was briefly at a standstill. The war was over, and for a while the machines would stand idle whilst the labourers learned a new kind of weaving. .

Instead, she had put the women and children to work making large medallions and panels out of canvas and coloured them with the blue dye she had obtained from woad plants, now growing in abundance near the stream. When each medallion was finished, the name of a local hero was embroidered onto the front of it in a coloured thread.

Banners, flags, ladies' hats and men's hatbands too were made in this way; Joseph proved to be clever with his needle, picking out the shape of HMS Victory in coloured thread on each of them.

An outsized wall hanging was made. Shells brought specially from Bridport and pieces of twine were woven in, and it was decided that it would be hung between two trees in West Coker square. Laurel was picked to make the wreaths that would hang around the heroes' necks.

Mary had heard that Will Browne would be arriving home with her son, and someone called Jim, but these men were not the only heroes. The names of men from the local militia from the first Somerset Regiment and the Yeovil Sub-Division had committed acts of bravery, and would join the names of the three sailors mentioned on a special roll of honour when they arrived home.

Barrels of beer adorned the bar in the Royal George, and tables had been set out in the square, ready for food that had been cooked by volunteers, Bess Hill being the most generous.

Mary worried that if it rained the only place that would be large enough to accommodate everyone would be the Manor, but that would mean talking to Squire Seymour. She crossed her fingers.

It was a cold, fine day when the stagecoach entered the village of West Coker the following afternoon.

Tom felt as if he was being enveloped in a little secret valley, protected by great trees and high sturdy walls that ran along the side of the road as they plunged down into Pack Hollow. At the bottom of the hill familiar clumps of vivid waterside willows bordered the lake in front of

Westlake House, and when he raised his eyes again there was St Martin's church in the near distance. He looked firmly ahead, determined for today, at least, to put all bad memories firmly behind him.

Will and Jim craned their necks for a better view, for no doubt Jim was looking beyond the High Street and the Wash towards Crewkerne, where he would soon be meeting his own folks.

Suddenly they were in the square, and now church bells were pealing, slowly at first, rising to a crashing crescendo, drowning the cheering. People ran from their houses, a mass exodus that appeared suddenly, as if some massive force had evicted them and they swarmed around the carriage as it drew to a halt.

Tom noticed none of the bunting, for there they were, his own little family; Rose, Ben and Emily, and his mother, standing huddled together, waiting for him to climb down from the carriage and throw himself into their arms. Now Bess came hurrying across the square towards them, casting an anxious eye over her shoulder towards the tables groaning under the weight of all the food she had arranged on them.

Tom was overwhelmed, crying tears of happiness as he hugged his mother and the children, but when he took Rose in his arms and kissed her, a lump rose in his throat and he vowed never to leave her ever again.

Rose reached up and tenderly stroked the angry scar, and he flinched. The wound hadn't healed properly and would need treatment.

"Thank goodness that's all it was," she said softly.

Bess hovered in the background until Tom approached her. Stiffly she held out her hand, and her handshake was firm.

"What a joyous occasion," she smiled. "Especially as it comes so close to Christmas. I knew you could do it, Tom. I'm so very proud of you."

Chapter 19

On the second of November, eighteen hundred and five, HMS Victory, partially repaired, sailed to England with Nelson's body on board. The voyage took nearly five weeks due to bad weather and Beatty, Nelson's surgeon, knowing nothing about embalming, placed the body in a large barrel of brandy, had it lashed to the mainmast of the middle deck with a marine guarding it night and day.

At Gibraltar, the brandy was exchanged for spirits of wine, being drawn off and renewed twice during the journey home. Victory arrived at Spithead on the fourth of December, and after discharging the crew at Portsmouth, the battle scarred ship proceeded to Sheerness at the mouth of the Thames.

Beatty checked the condition of the body, and was relieved to find that it was still in good condition. Carefully it was stretched out and the autopsy performed. The musket ball was retrieved, along with a fragment of blue cloth and a particle of gold lace from Nelson's epaulette. Then it was sewn up and wrapped tightly in bandages, placed in a lead-lined pine coffin along with his organs, and filled with strong spirits before being sealed.

Victory wended her way slowly towards Sheerness, where she anchored, and as she pitched and tossed on turbulent seas the two coffins were winched with difficulty onto her upper deck.

Later, in the flickering light of the great man's cabin, his corpse was lifted; soaking wet from the coffin, drained and unwrapped. After it was dried, it was dressed in shirt, stockings, waistcoat and breeches. A prayer was read, and then the corpse was placed in an elaborate wooden coffin made from the mast of the L'Orient, an enemy flagship that had been destroyed at the battle of the Nile. It was then placed in an outer lead casket and sealed.

Now the Victory sailed to the Dover Roads and then onto the Downs, where Captain Scott, distracted with grief for his friend and hero watched over his body. The coffin was covered with black velvet, lined with satin and gilded with emblematic heraldic devices and sent to Woolwich on the twenty third of December.

Tom awoke on Christmas morning with mixed feelings. The evening before he had asked Rose to marry him and to his delight she had agreed. They had been sitting talking in the parlour discussing the state of the sailmaking industry, and the forthcoming funeral.

That night he had slept badly, after all he had been through it was now the funeral that made him realise the short time people had on earth.

Nelson had died at forty-seven years old, not a great age, but he had left behind the woman he loved and a daughter. How long would he, himself live? And what would he have accomplished by the age of forty-seven? He wasn't poor, but he was a man of simple means. What could he offer Rose? Marriage was the obvious answer, but would it be fair to her? Maybe she could do better elsewhere. He would never be another Nelson; he would never be able to put his country before the woman he loved. He wasn't brave, or clever, or respected, even. He had tried to do his best for his country in the only way he could, but was it enough?

Rose came into the room, and seeing him sitting hunched on the end of the bed, laid her hand gently on his arm.

"What are you thinking, my love?" she asked. "You look very serious."

214

He looked up at her and smiled. "I was wondering if you were happy. I don't know whether I'm good enough for you."

Rose threw her arms around him and kissed him hard on the lips. And that kiss was more passionate than ever before.

"Does that tell you how I feel? If you're still not convinced, I'll tell you. Every night you were gone I cried myself to sleep. Ben and Emily missed you, and your mother walked about like a lost soul. Because of you, the amount of canvas sent to the Navy increased considerably, and Jack Hayward, the Naval Inspector, reported that the quality of the material used for the topsail was particularly fine. On top of that, you fought in a bloody battle that many would consider complete madness. So what else do you want, Mr Welland, sir? Are you not aware that you are pretty much a hero in our part of the country, and that I shall be honoured to become your wife?"

"Oh, Rose." Tom's eyes filled with tears as he took her in his arms and held her close. "May I remind you that it was you who managed the ropeworks while I was away, and ensured that I came home to a successful business," he whispered.

"Your mother had a lot to do with it, you know," protested Rose. "We didn't always get on, but we managed, and I think you should know how proud she is of you, Tom."

His mood changed in an instant. "I wish everyone would stop saying that," he snapped. "There's nothing special about me, I can assure you."

"There's still something bothering you, isn't there?" Rose sounded concerned.

"To be quite honest, my love, I'm not looking forward to the funeral. Thousands of people will be there, and when I meet the crew again it'll bring it all back, and that battle is definitely something I don't want to remember. The twenty first of October will be a permanent anniversary, not only for us, but also for the rest of Great Britain, and I shall have to do my best to deal with it. But because I need to say goodbye to the great man properly, I shall go and pay tribute. Today, I will try to make Christmas a time to remember for the children, to make up for being away from them for so long, and hope they'll be satisfied with the few presents we've managed to find for them."

Ben knocked once, and then poked his nose around the door. "Can we open our presents now?" he asked plaintively. "Em and me, we've been waiting for hours, and we're bursting with excitement. And we've got something for you," he added mysteriously. "But you've got to come outside to see it. Are you ready?"

"What about Rose?"

"It's for her as well, silly."

Tom frowned. Ben needed a father's care, that was all. He'd have all the time in the world now to teach him how to curb his cheekiness, to learn to be a man, and to enjoy being a brother to his new sister and son to his new mother.

And with that thought in mind, he decided to make sure he had a clean black neck handkerchief and stockings, and some crepe for his hat to wear with his seaman's clothes at the funeral, and went out into the yard to meet a new family member, an adorable mongrel puppy.

On the morning of the seventh of January a select group of seamen and marines arrived at Greenwich hospital and were received by Lord Hood at the North Gate near the river.

People were calling out their greetings and thanks to the men who had freed their country from the grip of Napoleon; the applause was deafening as they made their way towards the Painted Hall where Nelson's body lay, as they had been given special permission to view the coffin.

Tom could feel hundreds of eyes upon him, failing to realise that instead of being an embarrassment the sailors' wounds were the subject of sympathy and discussion, and when he looked back, he could see that black handkerchiefs were clutched in thousand of hands in an emotional outpouring of gratitude.

After Nelson's body had lain in state in the Painted Hall for three days, it had been escorted to a funeral barge, one of the Victory's own, by five hundred pensioners, many of whom had known their dead hero well. His chest swelling with pride, Tom had joined the rest of the Victory's crew as they pulled the barge up to Westminster, and when he had glanced behind him, he had seen that they headed a long procession of black-draped boats and barges.

Crowds had lined the banks of the river, despite a strong southwesterly wind, watching as ships lowered their colours to half-mast, as tolling bells and booming guns drowned their cheering. Lines of armed guards, volunteers and pikemen held back unruly and excited admirers, whilst parents dealt with cold, fidgeting children.

Everything had passed in a blur as he pulled harder on the oars, his senses pounded by minute guns tolling from the forts at Tilbury and Gravesend, gasping with pain as the wind assaulted his head wound, all the time wishing he was in the warm. After the coffin was landed at Whitehall steps, Tom had sighed with relief. He was tired, and relieved that the journey by sea, at least, was over.

The next day dawned bright and fine as crowds of people silently came to stand knee deep on pavements along the route, waiting for a glimpse of their Admiral. At noon the procession moved off to the toll of minute guns. Companies of Light Dragoons, Infantry Cavalry and Grenadiers lead the procession, followed by pensioners from Greenwich Hospital, then came the seamen and marines walking in pairs, their blue sailors' attire mingling with the red uniform of the troops. With black handkerchiefs around their necks, stockings on their feet and decorated crepe hats on their heads, the crew carried the white ensign that the ship had flown off Cape Trafalgar, now and then opening the folds to show the shot holes to their captivated audience.

As all the regiments quartered within a hundred miles of London, together with a battery of artillery formed in St James's Park, one hundred and sixty carriages were assembling in Hyde Park, and marshalled coaches were snaking their way across Piccadilly through Horse Guards to the Admiralty.

The body of Nelson in his funeral car, its front and back an eighteen foot high carved representation of the head and stern of the Victory, was accompanied along the Strand and Fleet Street by many of his friends, including thirty one Admirals, one hundred Captains, officials, noblemen and princes, the Prince of Wales, and every prince in the royal family, and close officers, including Captain Thomas Hardy.

The procession was so long that its head reached the cathedral long before the end had left Whitehall. With his shipmates Tom tramped wearily through the streets for three hours as the procession wended its way through London, accompanied by the slow beat of the Dead March played on pipes and muffled drums; in the distance the doleful tolling of a bell. Hats were removed and heads respectfully bared in a wave that sounded like a sigh of farewell as the funeral car approached.

Tom watched as six chosen officers from HMS Victory waited at on the steps outside St Paul's with the bannerolls of Nelson's family, and when the Duke of Clarence ascended the steps he stopped suddenly, and took the colours that were borne by the Victory's men. After conferring with one of Tom's colleagues, he burst into tears.

With pride, Tom helped to carry the coffin inside, whilst six Admirals held a canopy above them, Hardy and Blackwood carrying banners and emblems representing Nelson's victories.

Now the rest of the seamen ascended the steps, with officials divided and ranged on each side, according to their rank, and entered the church. Then army officers and the bearers of their banners entered the choir and stood near the door; officers of state, dukes and His Royal Highness, the Prince of Wales entered the choir, along with heralds carrying the trophies.

Within the communion rails, the Prince of Wales requested that he should stand as close to the grave as possible, and Tom, seeing the royal head bowed in misery, shed tears of his own.

A chandelier of one hundred and thirty lamps hung from the great dome, casting muted light over the ceremony, whilst thousands of mourners stood under the huge torn flags of the combined fleet that hung from the balconies.

Now Tom, along with several of his shipmates, and surrounded by naval officers and heralds continued to bear the coffin up the aisle to the choir, the Admiral of the fleet, Sir Peter Parker, walking behind the coffin. During the service an octagonal lantern was lit, and when it was over, hours later, a bier rose from an oblong aperture under the dome and the coffin was placed upon it. It had been planned that all forty-eight seamen were to fold the battle ensign and lay it upon the coffin, but now, in an emotional gesture, they rent a sheet of cloth from the flag and tore it to pieces, each man stuffing his share into his clothing.

At last the coffin was lowered into the crypt and laid in a black marble sarcophagus, and as it sank from view, Tom remembered the greatest man he had ever known.

Afterwards, Rose fought her way through the crowds and joined him as he left St Paul's Cathedral, and they walked hand in hand through the empty streets of London, making their way to the inn where their carriage was waiting to take them home.

BIBLIOGRAPHY

R.C & J M Anderson - 'Quicksilver : A Hundred Years of Coaching, 1750-1850' (1973).

Attwooll, Maureen Weymouth – 'An Illustrated History' (Dovecote Press, 1995.)

Bridgman, Rosemary – 'Weaving A Manual of Techniques' (Crowood, 1991.)

Broadley, A M – 'Three Dorset Captains at Trafalgar' (John Murray, 1906).

Deutch, Yvonne – 'Weaving and Spinning' (Marshall Cavendish, 1977).

Eastwood, Colin - 'The Burton Bradstock Book' (Winterborne Press, 1988).

Eedle, Marie de G – 'History of Beaminster' (Phillimore , 1984).

Gale, Elizabeth – 'Farmers, Fishermen and Flax Spinners (E B Gale, 1984).

Goddard, Frank West - 'Coker : An Indication and Guide.'

Godwin, Peter - 'Nelson's Victory : 101 Questions and Answers about HMS Victory' (2004).

Hayward, Arthur R.J.P. - 'The Manufacture of Sailcloth in Somerset' (from the Somerset Year Book, 1936).

Hayward, L.C - 'From Portreeve to Mayor : The Growth of Yeovil' (Castle Cary Press, 1987).

Hood, Dorothy Violet – 'Admirals Hood' (Hutchinson, 1942).

Nathan, Matthew – 'Annals of West Coker' (CUP, 1957).

Newbury – 'Great Road to Bath' (Countryside, 1983).

Oman Carola – 'Nelson' (Hodder & Stoughton, 1987).

Pocock, Tom – 'Horatio Nelson' (Bodley Head, 1987).

Pope, Dudley – 'England Expects' (Chatham, 1998).

Pope, Dudley – 'Life in Nelson's Navy' (Chatham, 1981).

Rousell M & Pittard D - 'Crewkerne in Times Past' (Countryside Publications, 1985).

Schom, Alan – 'Trafalgar : Countdown' (Penguin, 1992).

Whitlock, P – 'HMS Victory & Admiral Lord Nelson' Portsmouth Guide Pearce William book - RNMTC